William Osborn Stoddard

The First Cruiser Out

A Cuban War Story ; Visitors at Grampus Island ; and The Tale of an Oar

William Osborn Stoddard

The First Cruiser Out
A Cuban War Story ; Visitors at Grampus Island ; and The Tale of an Oar

ISBN/EAN: 9783337100568

Printed in Europe, USA, Canada, Australia, Japan

Cover: Foto ©Andreas Hilbeck / pixelio.de

More available books at **www.hansebooks.com**

The First Cruiser Out

A Cuban War Story

Visitors at Grampus Island

and

The Tale of An Oar

By

William O. Stoddard

Chicago and New York
Herbert S. Stone and Company
Mdcccxcviii

Contents

Visitors at Grampus Island

Visitors at Grampus Island

CHAPTER I

THE FIRST COMERS

"Well, no, Jim," said Dan, "there is n't just anything that can't happen at sea. Wait till you hear some o' the old sailors tell their yarns. It's most always what you didn't expect."

"Then I wish we hadn't expected any wind," said Jim. "We shan't get to Grampus Island at this rate. How did it get its name?"

"Grampus? Kind o' whale," said Dan. "I'll show you when we get there. There's a stove in the wreck-house that's on it. We can have the biggest kind of time on that island."

"Not without some wind we won't," said Jim.

3

"Well," coolly responded Dan, "there's always wind enough, if it's only blowing. Just now it isn't. Anyhow, yonder's the island. You can't see much of it from here, but the fishing's prime off the ledges of rocks on the ocean side of it."

They were in a stoutly-built yawl, rigged as a catboat; that is, it had a mast, stepped well forward, carrying a boom and sail. Their present difficulty was that all the wind they had started from the shore with had blown itself out and they were floating helplessly about upon the long, slow swells which came in from the ocean.

It was all the worse for Jim because, as had come out in his talk with Dan, this was his first look upon salt-water. He was a western boy, on a visit to some seaside relatives, and he had stepped into the Polly that morning brimful of an entirely new fever. It was the sailor fever, and it had made him feel as if, on the whole, he would like to be an admiral and command a man-of-war.

Nothing like a new experience, however, had come to Dan. He would have been as cool as a cucumber if it had not been for the hot July sun that was looking down upon him.

4

"CAUGHT A CRAB FIRST STROKE," SHOUTED DAN.

Jim stared across the water a minute or so in silence.

"That's Grampus Island, is it?" he said then. "All you can see of it from here is something kind of black. I wish we could get there and see what it is."

"Mostly sand and rocks," replied Dan. "You don't know how to row or we might pull for it. It would be awfully warm work—"

"Let's try, anyhow," exclaimed Jim. "I have rowed a boat."

Dan made several sailorly comments upon the kind of boat his landlubber cousin must have rowed in, but he consented to make a trial, and out went the oars, one to each rower.

"Ready, Jim? Now! Pull!" ordered Dan.

"Oh!" was the next thing he heard, and there was Jim on the bottom of the boat, behind his seat.

"Caught a crab first stroke!" shouted Dan. "Try it again! I'll show you!"

Try it they did, and before long the Polly was making a slow and seemingly reluctant advance across the lazy sea.

There was nobody living upon Grampus

Island to wait for new arrivals, but away off to the eastward, it could not be said exactly where, there was a little coop of a room. It was so small that it could contain only a bed wide enough for one, with room at the side of the bed for a fellow to get up and dress in. There were two beds, in bunks, one above the other. There was a closed door, but there was no window. Instead of one, there was a round hole with a pane of thick glass in a hinged frame, which was now swung back so that air could come in and so that a young fellow standing by it could look out.

"This is awful!" he exclaimed. "I've got to stay here in prison till I starve to death, or till the ship goes down and drowns me. They are all gone!"

As far as his eyes could see across the dull Atlantic surges, with no wind to ripple them, there was no sign of life except one solitary sea-gull.

"Captain and crew and all," he said, very mournfully. "They went off in the boats while I was asleep. I guess they must have thought I was with them, somehow. The masts were gone before I came in here and lay down. She was leaking, but they hadn't

6

given up pumping. I understand it now. They made up their minds she was going to founder, and so they left her. If something hadn't rolled against the door I could get out. It's no use pushing—but, oh, ain't I thirsty!"

He was a bright, hearty-looking young chap, with dark, curling brown hair, but there was the saddest kind of look in his eyes. He was brave, too, for there was no quiver on his lips when he turned and looked around the bit of a cabin, or rather "state-room," in which he was shut up. There was a stool in it, just now upset. There were articles of clothing. There were several cupboard doors on the side opposite the bunks. Everything that he saw was very simple and plainly made, without any attempt at ornamentation.

He now stepped to the door and tried it with all his might. It yielded for a few inches, with a motion of the ship, and then it closed again with a bang.

"It is something heavy," he said. "I guess it may be a loose spar. Wonder if she is really sinking? She rolls dreadfully!"

That was because she was not under steerage-way and was drifting along at the pleasure, so

7

to speak, of the billows, which were bearing her westward.

From various remarks which he had made, it appeared that the Kennebec was a fruit-trader, and had been to the West Indies after pineapples, oranges, lemons and the like, and that he had sailed in her for a trip to the tropics. She had been dismasted in a hurricane, and he, Jack Watson, had probably been overlooked all the more easily because he was not one of the crew. If Jack had now been out on deck he could have kept his footing fairly well, for the rolling and pitching motion of the Kennebec was slow and easy-going. It was somewhat regulated by the fact that her crew had rigged a spare sail to the stump of the foremast, and that some of the shattered spars and wreckage were still towing astern. That kept her before the wind, when there was any, but did not keep her from yawing about.

Poor Jack Watson!

There was nothing left for him to do but to pick up the stool and sit down on it, with his chin on his hands, staring at the open porthole.

"It's of no use," he said. "If a sail did come in sight there isn't any way for me to signal her. Captain Bates himself said he'd hardly an idea where that gale had driven us. He said last night that we were as likely as not to go ashore any minute, if we didn't go to the bottom first. They were a pretty badly scared lot of men.''

He arose and went again to the porthole to peer out. There was now a ripple on the surface of the swells, and a faint breeze was filling the bit of sail on the stump of the foremast. He was not thinking of that, but of something he saw away in the horizon. It was not a sail; it was the long, feathery cloud of smoke from the pipes of an ocean steamer, and he gazed at it wistfully.

At that same hour Jim and Dan, in the Polly, suddenly gave up trying to row.

''Hurrah!'' shouted Dan. ''Wind!''

''Not much of it,'' said Jim, his red face testifying to the exertion it had cost him to take his first lesson as a salt-water oarsman.

''Better than rowing, anyhow,'' exclaimed Dan, springing back to get hold of the filler-ropes. ''Jim! Haul on those sail halyards! Swing it out! Up with it! There! More's coming! Here we go! If there's anything I hate, it's rowing. We've lost half of our first

9

day, anyhow, but this'll take us to Grampus Island a-kiting.''

Now the calm was ended, it was fun enough for a land boy to be sailing along over salt-water for the first time in his life. The waves arose merrily, and the Polly went over them like a duck.

''Jim!'' exclaimed Dan. ''There's a shark-fin. Guess he's after bluefish. There were schools and schools of 'em around here.''

''Let's try for 'em,'' said Jim.

''Not now, with that fellow driving 'em away,'' replied Dan. ''Nothing spoils fishing like a shark. We'll fish enough after we get to Grampus Island.''

Jim watched the shark-fin until it disappeared. He saw, too, more than one fish of some other kind spring half way out of the water and go under again. It was grand! It made him and Dan tell all they knew or had heard about sharks, and all the while Grampus Island was coming nearer; that is, every tack the Polly made carried her so much nearer to Grampus Island.

There it lay, looking black and gray and desolate enough under the summer sun. There was not more than a half mile of it in length, and it arose at about the middle of it in a mass of pokerish-looking rocks that Dan explained to be the back-fin of the fish the island was named after.

"It splits, too, out at the southerly end," he said. "That's the tail. The head of it's nothing but one big ledge. It's a sandy beach on this side, but the weather shore is the worst kind of rocks. You'll see high breakers there. Awful place for a ship to strike. Some day or other there's going to be a lighthouse, but it isn't built yet."

"Let's get ashore," responded Jim, eagerly. "I want to go all over it."

"We'll land in the cove between the tail," said Dan, as the Polly went about for another tack. "That's the safest harbor for a boat. It's all locked in. A storm couldn't get at her."

He was captain as well as pilot, and Jim sat still, studying every point of the island shore-line while they glided along southward.

One thing was plain enough. Only fishermen or people on a picnic would ever care to visit that forsaken-looking patch of sea-sand and weather-beaten granite, sticking up there in the ocean, all alone by itself. If ever any trees had tried to live there, they had given it up; but there were a few scrawny bushes hiding along under the landward side of the rocky fin in the middle of the island.

"Here we are!" shouted Dan, as the Polly rounded the southerly point.

"Whoop!" responded Jim. "It's a reg'lar built harbor. There's the other half of his tail across yonder."

"It's the biggest half, too," said Dan.

They were running in now, and in a few minutes more the nose of the Polly was resting on the beach at the very head of the cove.

"We'll anchor her so she can't get away," said Dan; but Jim was looking shoreward, and he exclaimed:

"There's the house! What's it there for?"

"They put 'em up in lots o' places," explained Dan, "so that if a wreck comes ashore and everybody aboard isn't drowned, the saved people can get under cover."

"Out o' the rain," said Jim. "But it isn't much of a house. It wouldn't hold a crowd of passengers."

In that respect, at least, it was not at all like the great ocean steamer that was swiftly drawing nearer to the yawning hulk of the deserted Kennebec, with its one passenger cooped

up so securely in his hot and narrow stateroom. She was a splendid affair, a perfect
queen of the sea, and she did not care whether
the wind blew or not. There were brightly
colored awnings on her decks here and there,
and under these her passengers were enjoying
themselves in all sorts of ways. Some were
reading, some were promenading, some sat
still and looked at the sea and the sky, while
on one of the main decks a uniformed band
was playing and a merry dance went on.
They were not in danger. They had no need
for anxiety about their voyage or its safe ter-
mination.

Suddenly, however, word went around
among them that the lookout had sighted a
drifting wreck. It was one more event. It
might be something exciting, and every spy-
glass and telescope and opera-glass on board
the steamer was busily engaged by the eyes of
men and women who were curious about the
wreck.

Jack Watson had no glass, but his eyes were
busy enough. So was his heart, for it beat
very quickly now and then, while he watched
the steamer and saw it seem to grow larger as
it came nearer.

"They are coming!" he said. "I'll see if I can't swing a sheet out of the porthole. They might see it. They'll never go right by without finding out if there is anybody here. Maybe I won't be drowned after all."

He felt a choking sensation in his throat while he thought about it. His mouth was getting dry and husky, and it was only in a kind of whisper that he said to himself:

"I shall never see mother again if that steamer doesn't send a boat on board this wreck. It's my last chance."

The boys on Grampus Island were not thinking of anything in particular just then. They were not even talking. Jim left Dan to finish caring for the Polly while he himself hurried away up the slope for a look at the "wreck-house."

There was hardly anything to see after he got there. The door opened with a great wooden latch. Dan had told him it was wood, because iron rusted so fast in salt-sea air. He understood that better after he saw the big red-rusted stove in the bit of a cook-room back of the two large rooms of the wreck-house.

"A little more," he said, "and there won't

14

be anything but rust left. I guess one room is for men and one for women, and this is the kitchen. Lots of firewood, anyhow. Pots and kettles, too."

Something had really been done for the comfort of shipwrecked people, if any should ever come, but meantime it was also a good arrangement for fishermen from all along shore. Dan said they kept it in pretty good order, and they used it a great deal in stormy weather. All around the sides of the rooms were roughly-made, empty bunks.

"No beds in 'em," remarked Jim, "and some could sleep on the floor. I don't ever want to be wrecked ashore into such a hotel as this is."

"Come on, Jim!" just then shouted Dan, from the outer doorway. "The tide's coming in. It's time for you and me to be on the wind'ard ledge, if we're going to try for any haddock. I've brought the pail of bait and my tackle."

"I brought along mine and one of the dinner-pails," replied Jim. "We can go back after the other things by and by."

"All right," said Dan. "Come along. The wind's going down again. Queerest kind of weather. If it should come on stormy we couldn't cross to the shore for days and days. My folks wouldn't care much. They know where we are.''

Perhaps he was right and perhaps he was not, but he and Jim hurried away toward the easterly side, the ocean front of Grampus Island, well assured that no kind of storm could sweep away a place that so many storms had tried their strength upon ever since the island was put there.

On the deck of the big steamer the eyes and the glasses were as busy as ever, but they were not now quite so successful as most of them wished to be. On the very highest deck, well forward, stood a couple of men in blue uniforms. Each carried a telescope, but they were not using them.

''Captain,'' said one of them, ''I wonder how far that hurricane drove us out of our course. I believe the reckoning's wrong.''

''That might not be the worst of it,'' replied the captain. ''We're out of the track of icebergs, but, mate, what does that fog mean?''

''Looks like they might be around,'' said the mate. ''I never heard of a 'berg hereaway, but all sorts of things happen at sea. That fog's coming after us.''

The fiddles and the brass-band music and the dancing still went on. The steamer plowed her way majestically.

The sun shone brightly enough. Everything seemed to be perfectly safe and peaceful, but Jack Watson at his porthole in the starboard side of the helpless hulk of the Kennebec felt his heart sink within him. He had hastily pulled a sheet from one of the bunks and had folded it so that he could put it through the small, round opening. Then he shook it out and tried to make motions with it.

''There isn't wind enough to lift it,'' he almost groaned. ''Maybe they'll come near enough to see me swing it. What's that?''

He had been busy with his sheet, and now, as he again turned to look at the steamer, he could hardly see her. Something like a long, whitish-gray arm reached out across the water and held a veil of its own between Jack and the crowd of watching passengers on the steamer.

''Fog!'' exclaimed Jack. ''Why, they'd go right by me. Nobody could see the sheet, and I couldn't shout loud enough to make them hear.''

CHAPTER II

"Here's the place," said Dan, as he and his western cousin stood side by side upon a huge flat rock. "It's pretty deep water between this and that outer ledge, and the fish run in between 'em."

"There's no beach on this side of the island," remarked Jim, glancing up and down the long shore-line. "All rocks."

"Just now it is," replied Dan; "but there's beach enough at low tide. There are shallows away out, too, and sandbars. That's the worst of it, for the bars change all the while, and you can't tell where they are. They say it's all because of an ocean current along the coast; but how it works, I don't know."

Jim really did not seem to care, for he was busy with his rod and reel and a small fish from the pail that Dan had lugged along with them all the way from the Polly. The day itself was pretty nearly used up, for they had not set out from home any too early, and the long calm had wasted time for them.

Now, however, their fisherman's fun began, and there was plenty of it. Not that the fish bit very fast, nor that every bite resulted in a catch. Dan's first luck was a blackfish, and his next was a porgy, and Jim looked at them with a strong sense of envy as they lay flopping on the rock.

"There isn't anything like that in any of our ponds or rivers," he confessed. "But now and then we get pickerel bigger than that blackfish. They are first-rate eating, too. Hey?"

"You've struck something!" shouted Dan. "Let your line run out. Now reel in. Strike him! Pull hard!"

Jim followed his instructions a little nervously, but it did not require such very hard pulling after all, and he was almost astonished at the size and weight of the fish he at last drew out.

"A haddock won't fight like a bass," said Dan. "Tell you what, though, a bluefish o' that size would have cut out work for you. We've got to troll for bluefish if we're to get any. I never caught one offshore in my life."

Jim had to hear a great deal concerning the

19

fish of the Atlantic coast, and of the various methods of going after them; but all of a sudden the biting seemed to have entirely ceased.

"It's no use for us to sit here any longer," said Dan. "The tide's changed; it's pretty late, too. Let's go and cook some porgies. We'll put the rest into the fish-car, so they'll keep."

They were already "on a string," anchored in shallow water near the end of that ledge. The luck had been so good that the fishermen had two trips to make before they could settle themselves as cooks in the wreck-house. Just before they set out the second time Dan mounted the highest rock and took a long, inquiring look across the water eastward.

"What is it?" asked Jim. "I can't see anything. 'Tisn't a ship?"

"Ship? No," said Dan; "it's nothing but a streak of fog. All the fishermen said we'd have good weather after such a storm as that was. It's too bad; fogs don't stand for good weather around here."

"It won't hurt us, I guess," replied Jim. But Dan shook his head, and walked a little faster as they went to the wreck-house.

Nobody seemed to think well of the thick

mist which was sweeping along over that part of the ocean. Moreover, it was not a warm fog, and whatever it came upon grew colder rapidly. It had not come from the tropics. It lay heavier and deeper as the night came nearer, and it was already making a kind of damp, disagreeable night of its own all around the steamship Carnatic. She was now going through the water more slowly, as if she were feeling her way with care. Some of the passengers were below, but large numbers of them were still on deck, making remarks to one another about hurricanes and fogs and other evils of sea-traveling.

"Where away was that wreck?" asked the captain of the mate, when they met on "the bridge," the lookout-place above the highest part of the steamer.

"She must be pretty near us now," replied the mate. "I've made sure of not running her down. Hullo! There she is, to larboard! Nobody at the wheel! Been abandoned! No use."

"Whistle," said the captain.

Screech after screech went out from the steamship, but there was no response from the Kennebec. The fog had lifted for a moment, so that they could scan, with their glasses, every square foot of her bare deck. There was neither sight nor sound of a human being there. At least the officers and crew of the Carnatic said so. All the passengers said so, excepting one. She was an elderly, kindly-looking woman, who had been leaning as far as she dared over the rail on the larboard side, listening.

"I heard a voice!" she exclaimed; "I know I did. It was faint, but there is somebody on that wreck!"

"Nonsense, madam."

"Nobody else heard it."

"All your imagination, my dear lady."

There were remarks all around her, and she was just saying, "There, I heard it again!" when the voice of the captain rang out through his speaking-trumpet:

"Hard aport, there! hard aport! Down with her! Port!"

A thrill and a chill and a shiver ran through all who heard, and then there were loud screams, and men and women ran hurriedly to and fro, and the drifting hulk of the Kennebec was instantly forgotten. There she lay, however, with the white fog closing pitiably around her, the long waves lifting her as if to show her to any observers, and then pitching her down the next smooth slope of dark water.

Jack Watson's porthole and his white, swinging sheet had at first been on the side nearer the Carnatic. He had felt sure of being seen, even after the fog came, for he knew the steamer was approaching.

"I can't see her now," he said, at last. "I'll try to make them hear me."

He shouted again and again, but at first she was too far away, and sound does not travel well in a fog. He was just trying again, doing his best, when the Carnatic blew her whistle, and the discordant screech drowned his voice, as if it blew purposely every time he opened his lips.

"Oh, if they would stop whistling!" groaned poor Jack. "If they would, I could make them hear me. Must I be left here to die, and they so near?"

That was the hardest part of it. To have a hope come, and then to lose it altogether. He stuck closely to his porthole, staring out into the fog minute after minute.

"They may send a boat," he said; "if they

did, I could make anybody that came on board hear me. What's that? No, they haven't come! Oh, this is awful!''

The fog had seemed to kill what wind there was at first, but now a pretty strong breeze blew suddenly from the eastward, and it cleft a great rift in the fog.

''I thought I heard screams and shouts,'' muttered Jack. ''Has anything happened? She must be very near me now.''

The Carnatic might indeed have been much nearer the Kennebec but for the sudden order of her captain and the swift turns of her wheel. She had sheered away as if she had been frightened, and her engines were working at their best speed during a number of minutes. All was terror on board of her, and her rapidly lighted lanterns did not seem to be doing anything for the darkness in which she was plunging onward.

''There she is!'' exclaimed Jack, hoarsely, staring at a great dim something that surged along in the cleft of the fog. ''It's her! No, it isn't; it's something white. It isn't another steamer. How high it is! How it glistens! It's an iceberg! She must have gone right over that steamer. Then everybody on board of her has been drowned by this time.''

It was so terrible a thing to think of, that for a short time it almost made him forget his own situation.

''That iceberg missed the Kennebec,'' he said, aloud, at last. ''I never saw one before. But how this ship is pitching and rolling! What's that? It's right out there in the after-cabin.''

Whatever the sound was, it made him dart to his door and push. So suddenly did he shove, and so instantly did the door open, that he fell full length upon the floor. He was not hurt, and he sprang to his feet, exclaiming:

''I'm out!''

It seemed something like hope of rescue to get out of that hot little box, even into the cabin of a sinking ship drifting among icebergs. It was not so much of an improvement at once, for his next thought was, as he groped his way around, staggering with the rolling and pitching:

''Dark as a pocket! What I want is water. There's a filter at the end of the cabin. The lantern hangs in the middle.''

Another roll sent him halfway across. His hand went up to help him balance himself, and then he almost screamed:

"Lantern! I can hang on. Matches!"

He had some in a pocket, and in half a minute more the large swing-lantern of the cabin was lighted. Now he could go straight to the water-filter for a long, refreshing draught; but even as he did so, he remarked:

"It was that big sea-chest that slid against my door. It's open, too, but there isn't anything to eat in it. Hullo! The hand-lanterns always hung by the filter."

He lighted one of them next, but after he had done so he stood still and seemed to be thinking.

"They said there was too much water in the hold," he said. "She's leaking, but it hasn't got up as high as the cabin yet. She may float till morning. I'll go on deck. There may be something to eat in the caboose."

The waves were not breaking over the Kennebec. She was going along better, now that there was wind to fill her bit of canvas. She was getting steadier. The dense fog had wrapped her in, so that one end of her deck could hardly be seen from the other, but the

THE LARGE SWING LANTERN WAS LIGHTED.

moment Jack came up from below he knew that all her boats were gone. He was therefore all alone on board.

"I do hope they got away," he thought. "I wish I knew that none of 'em were drowned. They were real good fellows. Of course, they never really meant to leave me here. Anyhow, she isn't going down very fast."

They must, indeed, have gone in a hurry, for when Jack reached the caboose, the cookrooms, he found the boiler half full of cold boiled beef, and there was plenty of ship-biscuit in the cubbies.

"I'd have starved down there," he thought, "or else I'd have died of thirst, if I hadn't been drowned. It was just the most awful place to be in! I'd rather be drowned from up here, if I've got to be. I can hear and see what's going on."

There did not seem to be anything going on, and his one lantern was a mere speck in the dense darkness which had settled over the sea. Jack could sit in the caboose and eat all he wanted. Then he could go out and scout all over the ship, above and below. She was schooner-built, a first-rate sailer, of about six

27

hundred tons. She had carried some deck cargo, but every bale and cask of it was gone. All her hatches were closed, excepting the after-cabin hatchway through which Jack had come up. It was a good while before he cared to go down again, but he grew tired of doing nothing. Besides, it did him good to have even the small excitement of rummaging from place to place.

"I wouldn't steal a thing," he said, "but they hauled out lots of stuff that they couldn't take with 'em in the boats. The captain left one of his fine chronometer watches. It's running. I'll wind it up and keep it for him. I know where his wife lives. Guess she'd be glad to get it, whether he ever comes home or not. I hope he'll come. Go to sleep? I guess not. If I hadn't been so tired and slept so sound, I'd never have been left behind. I'll stay awake till morning."

That was not what Dan and Jim intended doing. They had made preparations for spending the night in the wreck-house. That is, Dan had made them, with some help from his mother.

"Only a blanket apiece," he told Jim. "She said she wouldn't make me too comfortable, and then I wouldn't care to sleep here more'n one night."

"Guess I can sleep anywhere you can," laughed Jim. "But what I want most is supper. The fire's going tiptop; we'll have coffee pretty soon. We've cleaned more fish than you and I can eat."

"Don't know," said Dan; "fellows eat like anything on an island like this. We'll get some clams at low tide, to-morrow morning. I like clams."

It took a long time to do all the cooking and eating required by that first picnic supper on the island. If ever any fish that were caught tasted well, it was those very fish. Dan had not made so bad a guess after all, but when it was ended he turned to Jim, and remarked:

"I don't want to go to bed yet, do you?"

"Not a bit of it," said Jim. "I'd rather take the lantern and go out."

"We wouldn't need one if it wasn't for the fog," said Dan. "The moon'll be out after awhile, but it's the darkest kind of night just now. Come on."

There was no danger whatever of their losing their way. They could not have wandered off from Grampus Island. Their first errand was to the Polly at her snug resting-place in the tail of the Grampus. There she lay, the fish-car in the stern of her, pretty well stocked with freshly-caught fish. She had been put together for precisely this kind of business, and she wore a stanch, sea-going look. No doubt she had had her experiences, if she could have told them. So, too, had Dan, and he enjoyed himself immensely, as they went along in telling adventure stories of what he had seen and done. He had once been out in a mackerel-sloop. He had been "off the banks of Newfoundland" for days and days with that smack. Again, he had gone in another craft after codfish. He also promised Jim loads of fun after they should get ashore, in going with the fishermen to see them haul the seine-nets.

"They'll go almost anywhere in such a boat as the Polly," he asserted. "Now, let's go on along the shore and away around. We needn't break our shins against the rocks if we keep a good lookout. But what a fog this is!"

There was really nothing at all but fog to be seen on that side of the island. As the wind was easterly, what there was of it, that was the leeward shore, and there were no rollers coming in along the sandy beach. Hardly, however, had the adventurers worked their way around what Dan called the "fluke" of the Grampus, the tail-end of the island, before they discovered a very different state of affairs. Jim had expected a surf, for he had all the while heard the thunder of it as the Atlantic billows came surging in among the rocks or broke along the strand. What he learned now was that the worst breakers were not close inshore, but away out at some distance. It had been so at the ledge where he and Dan had fished, but there was no outer ledge here, and the breakers he could now hear, but not see, were out upon a sandbar at some distance from the island. They seemed, too, to sound louder at night than they had in the daytime, or else they were larger waves.

"Hark!" exclaimed Dan, suddenly. "Keep still for a moment. Listen! Didn't you hear it?"

"I heard something," said Jim; "I thought it was the surf."

"Surf? No," said Dan. "Wait. There it comes again. Jim, it's a signal-gun! Come on. We must start a fire on the back fin.

There's a stack of driftwood there all ready to kindle. Look out, though, it's rocky."

"Signal-gun?" said Jim, the first chance he had to put a word in. "Do you suppose a ship is sinking?"

"Why, no," said Dan. "All it means is that she's in distress. There ought to be a lighthouse on Grampus Island. We'll show a light, anyhow."

This was excitement enough. It was better than any fishing or picnic, and the boys made their way as fast as they dared to go among the fragments and boulders and ledges, all the way to the highest peak of the back fin of the rocky Grampus. It was flat enough when they got there—twenty feet long by ten feet wide— and as Dan had said, there were heaps of wood lying around, brought there with laborious care to make a beacon with in case of need.

"Not too much of it at once," said Dan. "There goes that gun again! If it wasn't for the fog, a fire up here could be seen from miles away at sea. Pile it on. That's a tar-soaked chunk. I've cut some splinters; hold your hat down over 'em. It's going. Careful, now."

Up sprang the bright blaze, rapidly catch-

32

ing the dry pine sticks and then the heavier pieces of oak plank.

"It comes ashore on the island," said Dan. "They chop it up and bring it here."

Jim was deeply interested in the beacon-fire, but as soon as it was burning well he turned to listen. "Boom!" Again and again had come the sound from the sea, dull, heavy, with something mournful in it. What could it mean? Who was firing it? What kind of distress were they in?

"Dan," he exclaimed, "I saw loads of driftwood down near where we were fishing. Let's go and light another fire; it might do some good."

"It might," replied Dan. "What a fire does is to tell 'em not to steer that way. Hark!"

Far away and faint, half smothered by the fog, sounded something like a shrill, hoarse scream.

"Come on, Dan," shouted Jim; "we must hurry down and start that other fire."

"We'll heap up this," said Dan, "so it'll burn till we get back. Roll on that piece of spar; it's pine. That's an old rudder-post; pitch it on. Hurrah! It's dancing up fine. That'll do."

33

VISITORS AT GRAMPUS ISLAND

They were almost gleeful over the success of what Dan called their new lighthouse business, but it was not well to be too hasty in climbing down from the fin of the Grampus. Every now and then, as they were doing so, they heard again those strange, warning sounds from somewhere out in the fog and on the sea.

CHAPTER III

AMONG THE BREAKERS

Strong and bright was the blaze which was now flaming up from the top of the granite back-fin ridge of Grampus Island. The pine spars and the oaken timbers burned well.

It was not their fault that they had so much fog to contend with, and in spite of it they made of themselves a pretty good substitute for a lighthouse.

The fog did not now reach everywhere. The strengthening breeze was forcing it to the landward, and there was one broad space out at sea where the light of the rising moon found nothing to hinder it.

"Boom!"

Out of the center of that open space there came a great roar, and the moonlight suddenly discovered a vast upburst of foaming water to pour its radiance upon. It was not an ordinary wave. No wind had manufactured it. No cannon had sent out that thunderous report. Great waves had indeed been rolling there, but at that moment they broke up and fled away in all directions, for they were exceedingly startled by something which had unexpectedly happened.

Probably not the oldest wave among them had ever seen that thing done before. Right in the middle of them all there had been towering a white giant of ice, floated down there from the far-off Polar sea. Hundreds and hundreds of miles it had slowly floated, melting and perishing inch by inch, as it wandered further and further from the strong frosts among which it had been born. All the while, moreover, through storms or sunshine, the broad ice-floe under it, that held it up, had been weakening, dissolving. Its weakest place was at the forefoot of the ice king. Now, at last, the weight to be carried became too great at that line for the weakened floe to bear, and it had split asunder.

It was this tremendous splitting which had sent out the great roar. Then the iceberg itself bowed forward, groaning, and fell with an awful plunge. It would have been a magnificent sight if there had been anybody there to see it. Even the moonlight, however, had only a few moments for looking, while the fragments of the old berg rocked and rolled upon the topping sea. Then the same wind which had swept away the first cover of mist blew along another as dense, and all was once more a foggy darkness over many a square mile of the face of the Atlantic.

At quite a long distance from the place where the disaster occurred to the melting iceberg, the wreck of the Kennebec drove slowly westward before the breeze from the east.

Jack Watson had wearied of rummaging around below with his lantern.

"I've found all sorts of things," he said to himself, "but I don't see any use they're going to be to me, with this old schooner sinking under me."

Nevertheless, there was real comfort in seeming to have something to do, and he went up on deck again in a somewhat more cheerful frame of mind. He even went to the wheel and tried his hand at steering a few minutes, but it was tiresome, useless work, and he gave it up. What, indeed, could be accomplished by steering? Steering where? The Kennebec was really going along well enough, thanks to the rag of sail on the foremast and the shattered spar that was towing astern. She might as well be allowed to go her own gait and take her own course.

So, making up his mind to let her go, he once more made his way forward, lantern in hand, and when but a few paces in front of the foremast he almost fell over something.

The Kennebec was a peaceful trader, and yet the exclamation which sprang to Jack's lips was:

"Cannon! I guess that thing could make itself heard!"

His own throat was now in much better condition for shouting, but here was a fellow with a throat of solid brass.

"The ammunition's in the captain's cabin," he said; "I'll get it out as quick as I can. She's a four-pounder."

The cannon was not there for war, but for use in firing signals and salutes. It was a pretty piece, only that the salt spray falling upon it continually had darkened it, in spite of an occasional polishing which it was accustomed to get from the sailors of the Kennebec.

Jack was now in the captain's cabin, and he knew where to look for the ammunition. All

38

he had to do was to break open a cupboard door with an ax.

"Guns, too!" he said, as he looked in. "I'll take out that double breech-loader and a lot of its cartridges, if it's only for the fun of it. I've seen 'em load and fire a cannon Fourth of July."

The cartridges for the cannon were all ready for use, but they were bulky, and he could take only a few at a time.

"She's going steadier now," he said to himself, as he reached the four-pounder with his load. "I'll fire every five minutes. It won't be minute-guns, though; I can't load fast enough for that."

He was an entirely green artilleryman, but he got his first cartridge in place after awhile. Then he felt a little nervous as he put on the cap and stood back to pull the trigger.

"Bang!" it went, and a faint tremor shook the deck of the Kennebec.

Jack stood stock-still, as if he were listening, although he had not the slightest idea of getting any immediate answer from the fog and darkness around him. He had the captain's spare chronometer in his hand, watching the minutes.

"One, two, three!" he muttered; "now I'll load her up again. Hullo! Hark! There couldn't be an echo away out here at sea."

Faint and far away it sounded, but nevertheless there did come back something like the ghost of another cannon report.

"That's something!" exclaimed Jack. "I'll try it again."

In went his second cartridge, and it was rammed home more rapidly than the first had been. He felt as if he had something to cannonade for, and the cap went on as if he were afraid of being too late.

"She's a roarer!" he shouted, as the signal-gun sent out its flash and its reverberation. "Just five minutes," he said, looking at his chronometer. "Now, let's listen."

Only one minute did he have to wait, and then there was no mistake about it; he had been answered!

"Load and fire away!" he shouted; "I'll let 'em know where to come."

There was genuine excitement in it—something like having a sea-fight with the chances against him and the enemy all around him, for Jack's enemy was the ocean itself, with the leak in the bottom of the Kennebec. It could not have been the worst kind of leak, for there was no perceptible change in her, and the cabin floor was still dry. He had not looked down into the hold, and he took its condition for granted.

Pretty soon he had to go to the captain's room again for more ammunition, and when he fired his next shot the reply that came was surely a great deal louder.

"Whoever it is, they're nearer," he said aloud. "I've hung up two more lanterns, but they don't amount to much in such a fog as this is."

Down on the seaward ledge of Grampus Island at that hour there was pretty sharp work going on. There was only one lantern, and the two workers had to come and go together; but they were having fairly good luck at finding driftwood. The worst of it was that some of it was water-soaked, and more was in pieces too heavy for them to carry over the rocks. Before long, however, they had quite enough to begin with, and they were cutting splinters when Jim remarked:

"That gun sounds louder sometimes. Guess they're putting in heavier loads."

"I wonder if they can see the fire on the

fin," replied Dan. "It's kind o' blurred by the fog. Let's light up this one quick! Jim! That's a steam-whistle! There's a steamer out there somewhere."

"I can hear it," said Jim, "but it's a good way off yet. Hark! That gun came from just where the whistle did."

It was all a mystery, but they understood that somebody was in danger, and was in this way calling out for help that they were not able to give. Jim was a landsman, and so he was "all at sea," while Dan took on the dignity and responsibility that belonged to him as an experienced coastman in the habit of handling a wreck or two every day of his life, ever since he was born.

"Tell you what we must do," he said, as soon as the fire kindled well. "We'll pile on all the wood there is here, and then we'll go after the Polly. If there's any kind of ship coming ashore, we've got to be ready to do something. The trouble is, we've got to keep inside of the surf-line. The Polly'd be rolled over and over if she got into any of those breakers. Drown us both."

"Glad it isn't stormy," said Jim.

"If it was blowing hard," replied Dan,

"WE'LL PILE ON ALL THE WOOD THERE IS HERE;
THEN WE'LL GO AFTER THE 'POLLY.'"

"there wouldn't be any use for the Polly on ⋆ that side of the island."

The fire they had left behind them was kindling rapidly, and the one on the back-fin rock shone out splendidly. They felt very well satisfied with what they had done, but every now and then, as they hurried along toward the tail of the Grampus, the wind brought to their ears, louder and louder, the hoarse screams of the steam-pipe, while at pretty regular intervals they heard the roar of the cannon.

"Jim," said Dan, just as they reached the boat, "that ship has two guns, and one of 'em's bigger than the other; it isn't as loud a gun."

"That's so," replied Jim, springing into the Polly. "Come on! We may get a chance to save somebody."

They did not feel like saying any more just then, but up went the sail and away sprang the Polly, with the lantern tightly fastened at her nose. It threw its light only a few yards ahead, but the blaze on the back-fin seemed to be above the fog now.

The only trouble about that was that it had not been kindled a little earlier, and that it had been mistaken for an altogether different light. One man in a neat, blue uniform, standing among several other men variously dressed, had freely declared that it had told him exactly where he was, when it had not by any means done so. He and the others were putting on more cheerful faces than they had previously worn, and he had sent out fresh orders through a speaking-trumpet at the very moment when a great shudder shook the deck upon which he was standing. Then there was a flash and a startling cannon report not many yards away; a fierce screech from the steam-whistle; an uproar of many voices shouting at once. But among them all, the only words that could be made out plainly were:

"We've struck!"

"Thank God it's on a sandbar, then!" exclaimed the captain. "The old Carnatic is plowing right in!"

His trumpet was at work now, and orders went out rapidly; but he and his officers were as cool as cucumbers.

"Surf, surf, surf!" exclaimed one of them.

"Breakers all around us! They're not heavy enough, though, to damage a craft o' this size. Hullo, there goes that other gun again! If that fellow hasn't been following us, and we've just led him ashore!"

Out of the darkness not far away did indeed sound a signal-gun, but not any steam-whistle. Instead of that there shortly came two small but sharp reports, such as might be made by letting off both barrels of a double gun.

The engines of the Carnatic had been stopped, and she was now motionless. She was standing straight up, with the breakers roaring around her stern and sides, and it could be seen that there was comparatively quiet water ahead of her.

"This is what that bonfire did for us," growled the captain. "I took it for Hook Island light, with deep water here away."

"This has been the queerest excursion trip I ever heard of," excitedly remarked one of the women passengers. "It was good enough, the first part of it, but then there came a hurricane, and then there was an iceberg, and here we are now, wrecked! Nobody knows where."

"I don't care," exclaimed another woman. "I'm so glad to get to the shore again that I don't know what to do. The ship can't sink through a sandbar."

"It was the iceberg that scared me most," said the first woman. "When it came I was listening for the voice I heard on that wreck."

"There wasn't any."

"I'm sure there was. I heard it. It almost seemed to me as if I knew whose voice it was. But then he couldn't have been there. Oh, how I want to see him!"

The other woman turned away, and the one who believed she had heard the voice stood near the rail and stared out into the darkness, from which, every now and then, the people on the Carnatic had heard the gun which had first set them to firing their own.

It had not sounded during the previous ten minutes, for the reason that it had no cannoneer to load and fire it. The one artilleryman of the Kennebec had left his gun and had again taken hold of the wheel. He did not know much about steering, but he had exclaimed:

"A light! I can see it every time the fog lifts. I'm going to try and steer for it. That other gun sounds a good deal nearer than it did. There! There's the light again! I'm headed straight for it."

He worked hard at the wheel, but he found that he could not change the course of the schooner very much. On she went, in an obstinate way of her own, with the great waves

46

following her and every now and then dashing over her stern.

"That looks bad," remarked Jack. "I'll take a look below."

Down he went, with a lantern in his hand, but in a moment more he was up again.

"The leak's doing it," he said. "The water's in the cabin now! She's beginning to go down faster! I don't believe she'll float till morning. There isn't a boat left. There isn't anything to make a raft of."

That was so. All the deck cargo had been swept away. There was not even an empty barrel nor a fragment of timber—not so much as an oar—to help him keep afloat.

"Life-preservers!" he had said at one time; but when he went to the companionway, where they were usually kept, he discovered that the crew of the Kennebec had taken them when they abandoned the wreck.

"What's a life-preserver, anyhow," he said, despairingly, "away out on the Atlantic ocean? All I can do is to bang away with that gun."

He did not fire so frequently now, for he could not go down to the cabin after any more cartridges. To be sure, he still had a number left, but he felt economical of them. After

47

each firing, therefore, all he cared to do was to sit down on the deck, with one arm over the cannon, and think how terrible it would be when at last the schooner should fill, and the water come over the deck, and she would go down, down, down to the bottom of the ocean, taking him with her.

"Oh, mother!" he exclaimed, "I'm so glad you don't know it! All you'll ever know is that I don't come home. But the Kennebec won't, either. If any of the crew get ashore, they can tell her how I was left behind."

The wind was blowing freshly, and the night was passing away, but it was still very dark when he arose, and said:

"I'll let her off once more. There's that light again; it isn't so far off as it was. I can hear the water wash around in the cabin when the schooner rolls."

The gun was already loaded, but he pulled the trigger listlessly, as if he cared very little about it. Off went the gun, and Jack stood still, listening. No answering report came back during the next minute, but another sound was in his ears.

"Breakers!" he exclaimed. "How they roar! I am driving straight for them. Now the Kennebec'll go down quick enough! What a whistle! That other gun again! The light! Another light! It's a bonfire! My shotgun!''

It lay near him, and he snatched it up, fired both barrels, and then threw it down again to walk forward and stand upon the prow of the schooner, peering anxiously out into the gloom through which the lights of the bonfire on the shore and the blaze upon the back-fin of Grampus Island were gleaming.

''The steamer!'' he shouted. ''I heard them! She has struck!''

CHAPTER IV

THE WRECKERS

"Here we are!" shouted Dan. "We've rounded the outer point of the fluke. The Polly's running fine, but you can't see a thing yet. How that steamer does whistle! There goes her old signal-gun again."

"Guess they put in plenty of powder," remarked Jim. "They meant to be heard along shore."

"Loads of fellows'll hear it," replied Dan. "Besides, all the shore folks can see the light on the back fin, and they'll know what it means. They'll know just where to come. Every boat they can man'll put out right away, for miles and miles up and down the coast."

"Will they make for the island?" asked Jim.

"Of course they will," said Dan. "Any number of 'em. There'll be a squad of the service men, too, from the nearest wrecking-station, but they may be too late to save anybody. Tell you what, we can't do much among those breakers."

"Some of the drowning people may swim out this way," said Jim. "Or they may have boats."

"Any kind of boat might get itself swamped among the rollers," groaned Dan. "Just see how high that surf springs! It isn't so bad further along the reef. Oh, dear! We can't get anywhere near that ship. She's stuck!"

So she was. The great majestic iron steamer, with her precious cargo of human lives. But at the present moment she seemed even to be quite contented about it, and she stood there without a quiver, while the great billows rolled past, not many of them throwing water across her decks. She seemed, however, to be becoming a starry constellation of lanterns, and one of these was a huge bull's-eye affair, like the headlight of a locomotive engine, and it was sending its vivid glare hither and thither in all directions through the fog.

The fog, moreover, was losing its hold, and the breeze was sweeping it away in flying masses, most of which went onward toward the mainland.

It was a positive pleasure to the passengers

of the Carnatic to have their stranded steamer lighted up fore and aft so very profusely, and some of them were saying so at the very moment when the mate on the bridge sang out:

"There she goes! Three lanterns! Red, white and blue! She is taking the breakers, head on. I can see her now. She is dismasted!"

The fog had cleared away between him and the Kennebec sufficiently for him to observe that much, but he had not noted the solitary form that stood near the stump of her bowsprit, facing, in a kind of silent despair, the white, foaming line of surf into which the helpless hulk under him was plunging forward. Perhaps the water was deeper there; but at all events, the Kennebec did not require so much, by a number of feet, as did the Carnatic. She went right past, therefore, almost in a straight line for the bonfire on the shore, or rather for the outer ledge that lay a hundred yards seaward from the rock where Dan and Jim had done their afternoon fishing.

The Polly was there now, between the bonfire and the ledge, and she was tacking to go back for another look at the stranded steamer.

"Jim!" said Dan. "Look! It's just as I thought it was. There are two of 'em. 'Tisn't a steamer, though. She had a gun, but she didn't have any whistle."

"I can see her!" shouted Jim. "She's coming! Hold on, Dan! Let's stay and see her come!"

"She'll strike in a minute!" shouted back Dan. "There!"

She had not yet struck, but Jack Watson, standing there all alone, heard the voice of the mate of the Carnatic hailing him:

"Ship ahoy! Hold hard! We can send you help right away. We're only stranded! What ship's that?"

Jack gathered in his breath with a strong effort and returned the hail.

"Schooner Kennebec. Only one man left on board. Sinking. Dismasted. I'm John Watson, of Brooklyn. Let my mother know—"

Crash! The hull of the dismasted schooner at that moment went in among the rocks, but the kindly-faced woman at the rail had uttered a long, wailing cry, and then the crew and passengers of the Carnatic and Jack, himself, heard her voice, through the night and the mist and the roar of the breakers:

53

"Jack! It's mother! I'm here! Oh, my son! My son!''

"Courage, ma'am! Courage! We're getting out a boat! He may be saved yet! We'll go right after him.''

It was the captain of the Carnatic standing near her, and there were, indeed, groups of busy seamen at all the steamer davits, getting the boats ready to lower. There had been, however, a serious question about dropping any of them among those breakers, and the officers had been inclined to wait for daylight. One boat only was to be risked now, and it was to be manned by volunteers, for the chances seemed to be that even a lifeboat would be swamped in a moment amid that boiling surf.

Crash again! For a great wave had lifted the hulk of the Kennebec and swept her forward, hurling her down upon the ledge with a concussion which threw Jack flat upon his back upon the deck. He sprang to his feet instantly, but under him were sharp sounds of a snapping and rending of planks and timbers. The prow of the schooner became a mere fragment in a few seconds, and the next surge threw it on into the blind darkness beyond the reef.

"Dan!" shouted Jim. "I heard him! I saw him!"

"So did I," said Dan, coolly. "She split all to pieces. Steady now, Jim. I wish you could row. Steer. Keep her head toward the waves, and we won't be capsized. Hullo! Hullo! Swim this way! Boat here! Come on! Shout, Jim! Let him know where we are!"

They shouted vigorously, but they had not been heard at first. Away down under the water, the thought in the mind of Jack Watson was:

"I'm drowning, but I'll keep my mouth shut as long as I can. I've got hold of something. It's going up! I'll stick to it! I won't drown if I can help it."

There was a ringing in his ears and a feeling of suffocation in his chest, but the rope's end he had gripped had been dangling from the stump of the bowsprit, and that piece of timber was rising to the surface, after its first heavy plunge. It had gone ahead also, and in a moment more there was a white face visible in a streak of dark water amid the mass of foam.

"The light! I see the light!" sputtered Jack, as he blew away the salt-water he had taken in when he first opened his mouth. "I can breathe, too. I ain't hurt a particle. Perhaps I can reach the shore. Hullo!"

"Hurrah!" rang back from the two voices in the Polly.

"He is there!" yelled Jim.

"Catch that rope!" shouted Dan, as he threw one toward the spot from which Jack's answer came.

"I've caught it!" came bravely back; but at that moment there were loud, exciting voices hailing them from the shore, and Dan exclaimed:

"Jim! Some of our fishermen, I guess. The light and the guns told 'em where to come. Now we'll have all the help we want."

"Aye! Aye!" he sent to the men on the shore. "Two wrecks! A ship and a steamer! Bring boats!"

But men who had left their boats on the other side of the island to cross over and find out what was going on had not brought any immediate help with them. It was all that Dan could do, after Jack was hauled alongside, to get him on board the Polly without upsetting her. Hardly had he done so before Jack exclaimed:

"IT WAS ALL THAT THEY COULD DO TO GET JACK ABOARD THE 'POLLY.'"

"My mother's on board that steamer. She's away out yonder!"

That meant both his mother and the steamer, but Dan replied:

"Of course she is. She's a big one, and she stopped at the bar. Your schooner didn't draw so much water, and she came right to the ledge. That's what broke her up. The wreckers'll 'tend to the steamer. Were there any more of your crew?"

Jack hurriedly explained to them the story of the Kennebec and the hurricane, while the Polly was running along through what was now the not very rough water between the line of breakers and the shore.

"Jim," said Dan, "we've got to beach this boat on this side of the island. We can't get her around the point the way the wind's blowing now."

"I say, though!" exclaimed Jim. "See that! Boat from the steamer! Hey!"

It was indeed the lifeboat that had put out from the Carnatic, but it was full of water. The brave crew of volunteers who had risked their lives in her were clinging to her as best they could, while the rollers carried her shoreward.

"They'll get there if they hold on," said Dan. "Give me the tiller. Hold hard now! Get ready to swim if we go over! Whoop!"

It had all become a great deal like a confused and stormy dream to Jack. There was hardly anything real about it, except a bump on his head from the stump of the Kennebec's bowsprit. Even now, as he sat there in the Polly, dripping wet and all but exhausted, it seemed to him that he still could hear the voice of his mother calling to him from the steamer.

"I wish she could know I didn't drown!" he groaned. "Oh, I wish she knew!"

He was not by any means safe yet, however, for they had the shore surf to get through. There were now many lanterns along the beach. The bonfire was blazing brightly, and somebody must have climbed the back-fin of Grampus Island, for the signal-beacon there was streaming up redder and higher than ever.

There was a vast deal of anxiety on board the Carnatic. Passengers and crew were all aware that the Kennebec had gone to pieces, and that their own lifeboat had filled with water before it had gone a hundred yards. They believed that its crew had clung to it, but there could be no certainty as to that, and the captain had forbidden the launching of another boat.

All the while the wind grew stronger, promising a gale, and the ocean surges were crushing with greater and greater force upon the hull of the stranded steamer.

"Madam," said the captain, reassuringly, to Mrs. Watson, "I feel better about your son. The forward lookout says he heard voices and hurrahs from near the place where that schooner struck. You see, if he was the only fellow on board of her, I guess they must have hooked onto him."

She tried to say something, but she had to give it up, and the captain hurried away to his duties, saying to himself:

"Well, I hope it is so. It'll give her some comfort just now. But I must say it's the slimmest kind of chance."

So it was beginning to look to Dan, the captain of the Polly, as wave after wave threw salt-water into her by the bucketful. It was what he called "a reg'lar comber," however, that came to her assistance. It took her up as if she had been a bit of driftwood, and carried her kiting up the beach, to be caught and held there by the strong hands of a couple of men who knew Dan, and who at once began to shout questions at him. Instead of any other answers, he shouted back:

"The lifeboat from the steamer! Throw 'em a line! They're right out yonder!"

The line to be sent was one that happened to be coiled up in the Polly. In half a minute more, with a stone at the end of it, it went flying through the air, to come down across the unlucky lifeboat. Six men of its crew were holding on outside, while the remaining two had still made out to stick within. It was one of this pair that caught the rope, and the next second he sang out:

"Got her! Haul away!"

Then he turned to his own comrades and roared at them:

"Howld hard, min! Grip yer livil best. We'll all git ashore, the noo!"

It seemed to them a little dubious, for holding on was hard holding; but the pull from the shore was steady, and not one of the half-drowned sailors lost his grip, as he might have done if there had been any other jerks besides such as were given by the billows. They were all under water half the time, but they could catch a breath whenever their heads came out again.

"Hurrah! Hurrah! Hurrah!"

The ringing cheers which announced the rescue of the lifeboat crew were heard on board the steamer, in spite of the wind, but they could not tell Mrs. Watson anything in particular about Jack.

"How'd you happen to get here so soon?" asked Dan of a man he knew.

"Haow?" replied the fisherman. "Why, aour gang was away up the coast at the seine, and arter the haul we sot aout fur hum. First, then, we thought as haow we heerd a gun. Then we sighted the light on the back-fin. Of course, we kem. We hailed that there bluefish smack, and they tacked back with us. There'll be all sorts o' help here by mawning."

Even while he said it Jim was staring at a faint tint of rose color upon some clouds in the eastern sky.

"Hurrah!" he shouted. "Bully! We'll have some sunshine before a great while."

"Hark!" replied Dan. "Hear that? It's a speaking-trumpet right here on the island. Whoop! It's the coast service men. They know what to do with a wreck. We're all right now.''

His fisherman friends had also heard the trumpet and knew what it meant. In the course of a minute or so their talk had given to both Jack Watson and Jim a great deal of information concerning the coast service. Then a party of sailor-like men, headed by an officer in uniform, came hurrying along the shore, hauling with them a' curious looking something or other on wheels.

''That's the lifecar,'' said Dan. ''They carry all sorts of things in it. That thing behind it is the mortar, to fire a lifeline to the steamer.''

The life-saving service crew had crossed from the mainland to Grampus Island in a steam tug, and a score of brawny 'longshoremen had come with them. It was now getting so light that they hardly needed to ask a question before they knew exactly what to do. Down to the shore wheeled the mortar, a kind of wide-mouthed brass cannon, and every eye was watching it, while the curious mouthpiece, full of cordage coiled, was fixed on. The officer took a careful aim for the Carnatic, and then the gun was fired.

It was beautiful to see how accurately, swiftly, that flying cordage unwound as it went, and how it came down across the deck of the steamer.

The passengers and the crew were watching it breathlessly, and when it fell they gave it three cheers. They all felt better, now that the sun was rising, but not many of them had faith and courage to agree with the captain when he said to them:

"All safe now! The steamer'll hold together, anyhow, but you can go ashore if you prefer to do so. We shall pull her off and float her again, but it may take us a week or so to do that."

Jim was remarking to Dan:

"I wouldn't like to be fished ashore through the surf at the end of that line."

"You wait," said Dan. "Next thing they'll do is to land a hawser. Then they'll run a boat on the hawser."

Jim had only a few minutes to wait before he knew what it meant. He saw a strong rope drawn ashore by means of the lifeline, and firmly fastened. Along that rope, or hawser, the lifeboat itself could be hauled back to the steamer, and back it went, with men in it.

Up came the golden sun, but still the wind was strong, and the waves ran high. All the beach in front of the ledge where the Kennebec had gone to pieces was now strewn with fragments, and Jack went to take a look at them. It had seemed to him impossible to stand still and watch the wrecking-crew any longer.

"Hullo!" he exclaimed, as he came to a heap of rubbish on the beach. "If that isn't my gun! It couldn't float. No, it somehow got wedged in with the ropes and those bits of deck. It isn't hurt a mite. I guess the cannon won't come ashore." .

Back he marched, with the gun on his shoulder, just in time to hear a shout.

"The boat's putting out from the steamer! You can't see who's in her. She's all covered with tarpaulins. Haul now, men! Don't let 'em go under water!"

That was too much to ask. The returning lifeboat did go through rather than over some of those surges. Nevertheless, the people in her were safe enough, and it was only a few minutes before her prow was out upon the sand and the tightly-fixed tarpaulins could be stripped away.

In the very prow of the boat as it came up the slope, rising nervously and stepping out first of all, was a tall woman. She glanced swiftly around among the crowd, and then she threw out her arms.

"Jack! My son! Saved! Saved!" she screamed, with a half-choking sob at the end of it.

"Mother!" he gasped. "Both of us!"

He sprang forward, but hardly had her arms closed around him before he asked:

"But, mother, how on earth did you happen to get here?"

"Oh, Jack!" she said, "I did get so lonely after you went away. Then I thought I'd have a summer sea-voyage, too. Shut up for a moment; I want to thank God that we're both safe on land again."

Everybody heard her, and all the hats came off; but in half a minute more the lifeboat was ready for another trip. She had brought the captain of the Carnatic and a crammed load of passengers on her, first. It was the captain's duty, however, to go to the mainland at once, in the tug, that he might communicate by telegraph with the owners of the stranded steamship and with other people.

"Mother," said Jack, "Dan and Jim saved my life. They pulled me into their boat."

"Oh, how I thank them!" she began; but Dan interrupted her eagerly.

"I guess, Mrs. Watson," he said, "you'd better have some breakfast. If you and all of them will walk across to the wreck-house, we can have hot coffee in no time. Lots and lots of fresh fish."

"That's it," said the captain. "Go!"

"Come along, mother," urged Jack. "You must be awfully hungry. I am!"

"Oh, Jack!" she said, "I don't feel as if I could eat. I'm so glad!"

Nevertheless, she went.

There was a great swarm of visitors on Grampus Island that day, for there was a steamer load of them from the Carnatic, besides all the boat loads after boat loads that came from the mainland for a look at the wreck and at the passengers.

THE END

A Tale of a Broken Oar

A Tale of a Broken Oar

CHAPTER I

THE SECRET OF THE ASH-TREE

Once upon a time there came a storm of
wind, and it swept across the rocky slope of a
mountain in Vermont. Half way down the
slope of the mountain there stood a young ash-
tree, rooted in a deep cleft of the rocks. There
was a wrestling-match between the wind and
the tree. It lasted through a full hour, and
then the wind gave it up and went away. A
score of times during the gale the ash-tree had
bent over until its branches touched the nearest boulder, but each time it had sprung back
again, proving how tough it was. Then all
was over, and there seemed to be no trace left
of the power of the storm except that the tree
was not so straight as it had been.

Long years after the battle on the mountain
in Vermont there came a summer day upon

the sea. It was one of those days when the light wind ripples the water only enough to make it beautiful and to fill the sails of ships, enticing them to spread all their canvas. Then they look their best, being in full dress.

Those are also steamer days, but most of all they are the right kind of days for small boats, when they can venture safely away, far out from the shore.

Only one such boat was in sight, but there were a number of white sails in the distance. It was what is called a lapstreak boat, planned for two, or even three, pairs of oars. A round hole in the forward seat, and a socket on the bottom under that hole, were provided for a mast, if anybody wished to turn the rowboat into a sailboat. There was no mast in her now, however, and only one pair of oars was going. These were handled by a strong-looking young fellow, whose blue flannel shirt with white trimmings and his natty tarpaulin hat gave him a sailor-like appearance. His hands and face were not sufficiently sunburned, however, and he was already further from land than any weatherwise mariner would have wished to be in such a boat, even on so seemingly fair a day.

There were fleecy clouds beginning to gather in the eastern horizon, and the noon was long past.

"I guess I'll pull in my line," he remarked. "The fish won't bite. Only four bluefish in all day. Hullo, porpoises!"

The four finny prizes on the bottom of the boat were of respectable size, but they were mere minnows compared to the fat, jolly-looking "sea-pigs" that he could see frolicking in all directions around the boat. They paid it no more attention than if it had been another porpoise of a different kind, lapstreak built, but still one of themselves.

"If one of 'em should bite, I couldn't pull him in," remarked the young fisherman. "They're not good eating, anyhow. I don't know what they are good for, but there's fun in 'em. See them plunge around!"

There was some amusement in watching the porpoises, but the trolling-line was now in and coiled up, and the boatman was at his oars.

"Never thought of it!" he exclaimed. "I'd no notion I was so far out. Why, I haven't rowed all that distance!"

Perfectly correct. He had rowed only a small part of it, and a swift surface current of the ocean had done the rest. It was even now bearing him seaward at a rapid rate, and the shoreline to the westward was getting dim.

"There'll be plenty of daylight to row back in," he remarked; but he said it with a very sober face, and he added, "Longest kind of pull, though."

He had squared himself upon his seat and was prepared to do his best. A taller man with longer arms could have done much better, evidently, and two men on each seat would have manned the boat correctly. Pull he did, however, showing tiptop muscle.

Snap!

There was a cracking sound at the left-hand rowlock, a pair of heels in the air, and the rower lay on the bottom of the boat holding in his left hand only about a foot and a half of that oar.

It had seemed a good enough piece of wood. Other fellows had rowed with it many a time, but it had gone to smash at the weak spot that was made in the ash-tree by the hurricane on the Vermont mountain-side. He scrambled to his feet, and stood up as well as he could in the rocking boat, exclaiming:

"This is awful! Only one oar to get home with! 'Tisn't my fault, but what on earth'll become of me?"

No, it was not his fault. It was to be charged away back, years ago, to the hurricane; but for all that, whatever was yet to happen to him upon that sea-voyage would belong, in one way or another, to the curious story of the broken oar, and to the hidden defect in the ash-tree and its timber. He said as much several times over, while he worked with his remaining oar to keep the head of the boat to the waves, that it might not rock so unpleasantly.

"Glad nobody at home can know about it," he said, aloud. "They know I mean to stay a week at the seaside." He said enough more to indicate that he was from quite a distance inland, but at that very hour the keeper of a boathouse near a seaside hotel was answering a question.

"Yes'um. He said his name was Ned Anson, and he boarded at your house, not at the 'otel. 'E's been out all day, mum. The boat's as safe as a church."

"I wanted to know," she said. "He may not know how to manage a boat."

73

"Well enough, mum, for this sort o' weather," replied the boathouse keeper. "I saw 'im 'andle 'er, and she's werry easy to 'andle."

So good Mrs. Tompkins went back to her house, not altogether satisfied in her mind, but unable to say or do anything for her absent boarder.

As for Ned himself, he was anything but easy, and he now found his pretty, buoyant lapstreak wherry by no means easy to handle. She was inclined to be saucy at any time, and her very name was "Whistler," which is a good enough name for a boat, but it had nothing to do with the long-drawn, melancholy whistle of Ned as he sat and stared at his broken oar.

"If I had a mast and sail now," he was thinking, "I could do something. It's about the tightest place I ever was in. She's a good enough boat, but—"

He put his hand quickly to his hat-brim at that moment, for a puff of stronger wind had unexpectedly arrived. Not only was it stronger, but it came from the westward, and it at once took hold on the Whistler, all it could touch of her, and began to help the current that was bearing her out to sea. Wind and water were therefore in partnership against Ned, and he had only one oar to fight them with.

All around him rolled and rollicked the school of fat porpoises, keeping him company as though they enjoyed having him there, and were willing to cross the Atlantic with him. He could hardly see the shore now, only the highest points of it remaining above the horizon. Every time he went down into the trough of the waves and came up again, the first thing he did was to send a swift glance westward after the continent of North America that was floating away from him. The next thing was sure to be an anxious look in all directions for sails, to see if any were drawing nearer. They were not. On the contrary, every white wing among them appeared to be flying in some other direction, and the Whistler, with Ned Anson working his one oar at her stern, was dreadfully alone. She had a rudder, but there was no use for that just now.

Down sank the sun, and the long, swinging roll of the great ocean billows was becoming something terrible.

"They'll roll the Whistler over and over

yet," groaned poor Ned. "I can hardly keep her head to them. They're beginning to show bigger whitecaps, too. Just a wash of one of them into the boat, and it'd be all over with me."

As the sun went down the moon arose nearly full, and the glittering ocean grew very beautiful, but it seemed to Ned that it was also getting angry and preparing to drown him.

"Sail!" he suddenly shouted. "That's a sail! I know it is! I'll try if I can steer so they'll see me as she tacks this way. That's my last hope."

He was sculling with all the vigor he had left, but his day's work had been long and he was tired. About all he could do was to prevent the Whistler from being upset by the roughening waves which were dancing in the moonlight. There was plenty of that, and it was indeed shining on a sail that was rapidly nearing, or else the Whistler was drawing near the sail. It was a pretty large one, a kind of jib-sail; and behind, rather than under it, there lumbered along through the water a huge black mass that bore the shape of an ocean steamer.

Every such vessel has tall smoke-stacks

76

amidships, and something like them could be seen, but they were bent and battered, and there was no smoke rising from them. Not one solitary lantern was shining on her from stem to stern. There were no boats upon the davits. What had once been the cabins on the upper deck were splintered and torn, and only the foremast remained standing to help the bowsprit carry that solitary sail. No men or women walked the decks, but something or other that was living flitted back and forth, hither and thither, as the great iron bulk plunged slowly and steadily onward.

Before long it was evident to Ned that the course he was forced to follow by the drift of the current and the driving of the westerly wind was taking him right across the course followed by the strange sail upon which all his hopes and fears were centered.

"She might go by, or I might," he thought, "or she might go right over me. I could hardly get this boat out of her way. Why doesn't she hang out a light? It's a steamer, a big one. I can see that. They never stop for anybody, but she's going slow—about as slow as I am."

It was a time of terrific anxiety, and the

77

waves were surging around him as if they feared lest he might get away from them. All the porpoises had disappeared, and in place of them Ned had more than once seen what he took for the black back-fin of an enormous shark.

"Wonder if he's waiting for me?" thought Ned. "I'll do all I can to disappoint him, anyhow; but I'm almost near enough now to hail the steamer."

On she came, and on went the Whistler, and it was hard to tell which was traveling the more slowly. The Whistler, however, rode the waters like a duck, while the steamer rolled and pitched badly, and seemed to labor hard in coming up from the troughs of the long sea. She was pretty deep in the water, as if heavily laden.

"Ship ahoy!" shouted Ned. "I want to come abroad!"

No answering voice came back to him, and again he shouted; all in vain.

It was a first-class mystery, but nearer yet drew the cockleshell of a lapstreak wherry to the floating wall of iron, that looked larger than it really was in the glimmering moonlight.

"I'll get aboard if I can," gasped Ned, sculling his best. "I can see a rope ladder hanging down the side. If I can get hold of it I can scramble up. I'll keep hold of the Whistler, too. I don't want to lose her."

It looked like an awfully dangerous undertaking, and so it was; but Ned's affairs were desperate, and he had no choice but to scull straight for the side of the steamer. He had no more breath to shout with, and he thought he saw the fin of that shark within twenty feet of him. A cloud came over the moon, but he still could dimly discern the dangling rope ladder. A roll of the steamer toward him threw the ladder out, and he grasped for it.

"Not quite!" he said. "I must wait till she rolls again. This swell may carry me under. Oh, there it comes! Now! Hurrah, I caught it!"

It was not time to hurrah yet. He had indeed grasped the rope ladder with his hands. In a moment more his feet also were upon it, and he had kept hold of the line from the boat, but as the steamer rolled back again he was hurled against her with a force which almost made him let go.

"If I do I'm lost!" he exclaimed, between his set teeth. "I'll stick!"

Stick he did; and as soon as his grasp was firm again, he went up several rounds. Another roll of the ship did not bang him so badly, and half a minute more of desperate climbing brought him to the rail. He seized it with his hands, and at the same moment he heard a kind of shrill scream close to his right ear. It made him shiver all over, but he held on hard, and then tumbled in upon the deck. As he did so he glanced, half-frightened, over his right shoulder, but he did not see anybody, and he heard the same kind of shrill outcry from among the shadows cast by the remnants of the cabin. It was at that very instant that he noted how shattered was all the woodwork, and how bent were the smoke-stacks.

"Wreck!" he yelled, in real fright. "All I've done is to get on board a wreck! My boat? Yes, there she is! I must pull her up or she'll be stove to pieces."

The Whistler was already half full of water, but Ned managed to gear her line to one of the small windlasses at the davits. It was not beyond his strength then to hoist her prow, but he saw that that would only send her stern under. He must have been an inventive genius, for he swiftly made a slipping noose at the end of another line, left hanging at the windlass. He cast that noose over the stern of the Whistler, the other windlass was quickly at work, and then the jaunty shape of the lap-streak wherry, all uninjured, dangled at the rail of the mysterious steamer.

"I'm pretty nearly all right now," said Ned, "but this is awful! When I was on the ladder I thought I saw an ugly face looking down at me over the rail. There is somebody on board. Whoever it is he can't be afraid of me. Hullo! Where are you? What ship is this?" he shouted at the top of his voice.

It was not a scream this time that answered him, but a very low, faint kind of chattering, not one word of which could he understand. At the same time he believed he again saw something moving away back upon the roof of the shattered cabin.

"The Whistler's as safe as I can make her just now," thought Ned. "Seems to me I daren't venture any further on board this ship. Not till I can see somebody. I don't know which way to go in first. I'll push along toward the prow, and see if there's anything ahead of her that she might run into."

He said that because he thought he had

discerned a light somewhere to leeward just before he sprang for the rope ladder, but he was by no means sure about it.

There were stateroom doors open as he scrambled by, but all the moonlight was on the other side, and he could see nothing distinctly when he glanced in. He arrived quickly upon the forward deck, and he looked up at the great jib-sail. It was quite enough to keep the head of the steamer nearly right with the waves without any steering, and her clumsy weight did the rest, for she was going along steadily.

"There is the fore hatchway," thought Ned, "but it's closed and is covered with tarpaulins. That was to keep the water out. This ship has been through the worst kind of storm; there's no doubt about that. Banged her half to pieces."

It was battered pretty badly, all that showed above her iron hull. There was a door on which the moonlight shone in the middle of the cabin woodwork near him, and Ned went to it. The knob turned in his hand, and the door opened. He shuddered as he looked down a flight of stairs.

"THERE WAS A QUEER, HAIRY, LITTLE FACE ALMOST IN FRONT OF HIS OWN."

"Dark as a pocket!" he exclaimed, trying in vain to penetrate the gloom.

Then he shivered worse than ever, for a very small, cold hand took hold of his own, and then he felt something climbing swiftly up his arm.

"Gyp! Gyp! Gyp!"

"Yah! Oh! Hey!" yelled Ned, but there was a queer, hairy, inquiring little face almost in front of his own, and his next exclamation was:

"Monkey? Why, yes, a monkey! Are you the only fellow left on board?"

A rattle of shrill chattering replied to him, as if his climbing acquaintance were trying to explain matters, but Ned's fright was gone.

"All the other sailors went away and left you, did they?" he said. "Well! I'd never have come aboard this wreck if that oar hadn't busted. That's what brought me here. And now I'm at sea with a monkey on the biggest kind of steamer."

There sat Ned Anson at the foot of the cabin stairs all in the dark with the monkey in his lap, clinging to him as if he were afraid of letting go of his newly-arrived human protector. He chattered a little now and then, but the tone of his small voice sounded as if he felt very sorry about something. Whatever it might be, it was out of his power to explain. Ned, for his own part, was really glad of company, and he felt the effects of his long pull of rowing, first with two oars and then with one. He did not care to go a step further just then, and almost before he knew it he had leaned back upon the stairs to rest. Then he fell asleep, and Gyp, as he was beginning to call the monkey, nestled close to him and seemed also to be slumbering, while the deserted steamship rocked them slowly to and fro and plunged along across the Atlantic surges.

On land there was a light burning in the

boarding-house kept by Mrs. Tompkins, but that good woman had long since given up waiting for Ned.

"I can't sit up for him," she had remarked to another boarder. "If he was going to be gone all night, he ought to have left me word. Boys are keerless about sech things."

"Do you s'pose anything can have happened to him?" asked the boarder. "His folks ought to know."

"Mr. Lancashire, at the boathouse, says he's safe in this kind o' weather," replied Mrs. Tompkins. "I don't know jest where his folks live, but I can find out, if he doesn't come back to-morrow or next day. I ain't a-going to scare 'em half to death till there's good reason for it. I've had sech things happen before."

Probably not. Never in her experience as a seaside boarding-house keeper could she have had a crack in a young ash-tree in Vermont lead a fellow like Ned to go asleep on a deserted steamer with a monkey in his lap.

Gyp was awake first, and he began to stir as soon as a faint glimmer of daylight came down the stairs to say that the short summer night was over.

At first he only chippered gently, and looked around him. Then he got down and went up on deck; but he quickly returned and began to pass his small hands over Ned's face, chattering loudly.

"Hullo!" exclaimed Ned, throwing up his arms and trying to rise.

A pitch of the steamer threw him back again, but it awakened him thoroughly, and he began to remember what had happened.

"Gyp," he said, "it's daylight. What on earth are we going to do next?"

Gyp sprang away a few yards into the cabin, and then stopped, looking back, very much as if he expected Ned to follow him.

"That's what I'll do," said Ned. "I want to see what's inside of this ship."

At that instant he heard something, and it was not any chattering from the monkey. It was faint, smothered, but it sounded like a long, moaning, despairing cry.

"Hey!" shouted Ned. "There's somebody in there, away back. I can see pretty well now. Hullo! There's a water-cooler. Cup, too. Oh, if I ain't thirsty!"

The water-filter stood in the usual place for such things, at the forward end of a long, narrow saloon, on either side of which were ranges of closed stateroom doors. The carpet on the floor of the saloon did not seem to be wet. Ned noticed that while he was filling the cup.

"The steamer's had a rough time," he thought, "but she may not be sinking, after all. I'll go right away and see what that is. I'm coming, Gyp. Go ahead."

The monkey seemed to understand him, but he came back and looked up at the cup in Ned's hand.

"Guess he's thirsty," exclaimed Ned, and in a moment more Gyp was busy with the cup, holding it himself as if he were used to it.

"All right, Gyp?" asked Ned. "I'll take a cupful with me. Somebody else may need some."

He was glad he did, right away. Gyp led him on, holding one of his hands, and pulling him all the length of that saloon. At the further end of it a stateroom door stood open, and out of that room sounded a kind of whimper.

"I'm coming," said Ned, and the whimper changed to a short, gruff voice that made Ned almost jump.

"Dog!" he exclaimed. "There's a dog in there, and he's trying to bark."

The effort was a complete failure, but when Ned hastily rushed in, an enormous St. Bernard dog that lay on the floor half arose, fell back again, and languidly wagged his bushy tail.

"Water!" said Ned. "That's what he wants."

Down he dropped beside the St. Bernard, lifted his head, and held the cup so that the poor fellow could lap from it. He was answered by a whine of delight, and while the thirsty animal lapped away, Ned read upon a broad silver collar around his neck, "Roland von Arnheim, Hamburg."

"That's his name and his owner's name," thought Ned. "I can fix him up. Guess he wants something to eat. So do I, and so does Gyp. There must be plenty on board such a ship as this is."

The cup was empty now, but Roland could stand up, swaying a little, while Ned went back for more. He and Gyp drank again, and then they returned to the St. Bernard. Ned unbuckled the chain attached to the dog's collar, and while he was doing so Roland licked his face and hands, and seemed to be trying to say, "Thank you, sir."

Gyp had disappeared, and when Ned turned away to go after him, Roland was able to follow. He looked gaunt and weak, but his worst difficulty had been want of water.

The monkey had gone far forward, and he again was waiting at an open door. It was the door of the cooking-room, or kitchen, of the steamer. The moment Ned went in he understood it all, for in every direction were cupboards and drawers.

"Loads of things in them, of course," he said. "There's the range, too. I'll kindle a fire first thing."

The coal and kindling were right there, all dry and ready. It was easy to get the fire started, and as soon as the blaze sprang up Ned began to rummage in the cupboards.

"That bread's as dry as a bone," he said, "but I can soak it. Ship-biscuit. I'll soak some for Roland and Gyp. Plenty of water in this cask."

Gyp was ready for a plate of wet ship-biscuit, and so was Roland, but Ned worked on with a cracker in one hand while he explored further.

'No danger of starvation, anyhow,'' he thought. "But I'm going on deck. I want to see about the Whistler.''

His two comrades did not follow him at once, for they were busy, and he was all alone when he made his way to the larboard side of the steamer, where he had clambered on board. There at the davits hung the Whistler, and Ned's first remark was:

"I don't see how I ever managed to do it. I couldn't do it again. A fellow'll do almost anything to keep from being swallowed by a shark. I saved the boat, too, but those are tiptop windlasses. They'd lift the heaviest kind of boat. Hullo!"

He had just caught sight of his four bluefish, huddled together under the stern seat of the Whistler, and the next time the roll of the ship brought them near enough he secured them all.

"Fresh fish for breakfast," he remarked. "I guess a starved dog and a monkey can eat almost anything. I'll try 'em with fish.''

Before taking them down to the caboose, however, he felt himself bound to know more about the wreck. He already knew, from the gilded lettering over the cabin doorway, that the steamer was the "Dantzic," and that she hailed from Hamburg.

"So does Roland," remarked Ned, "and so does Gyp, probably. They'll do first-rate, soon as I can feed 'em up."

The sun was just risen, and the sea was quiet. There was no apparent cause for immediate anxiety, and Ned went over the steamer from end to end, taking note as he went of the large amount of breakage.

"Glad I saved the Whistler," he thought. "She's the only boat on board. What on earth's coming I don't know. Can't guess where I'm going, either, but I'm out of sight of land. Not another sail anywhere."

The wind was still westerly, and the Dantzic was making what headway she could farther and farther from the land Ned had left behind him when he set out in the Whistler. He had now finished his first observations on deck, and he went below. When he reached the caboose and looked in, there lay Roland, his head between his paws, watching the range as if it gave him a hope of better times, while Gyp sat gravely beside him, holding in one hand a tea-spoon.

"Hurrah, boys!" said Ned, "we'll have something worth while now."

An entirely new sensation came to him the moment he began to clean one of his bluefish. Up to that work had been too dreadful altogether, but there it suddenly seemed to change into a strange, wonderful but really splendid picnic at sea.

"It's the kind of adventure you read about," he remarked to Roland, throwing him a slice of raw fish.

"Woof!" replied Roland; but the bit of fish disappeared instantly, and he arose to be ready for more.

"There!" exclaimed Ned a moment later. "Who'd ha' believed a monkey would do that? I was going to cook it for him."

Gyp was quite ready to prove, however, that people of his kind can dispense with a kitchen. They usually do so at home, and he was not at all particular just now.

After that the sense of having a good time grew stronger, especially after the coffee was ready and a broad cut of bluefish came from the gridiron to a tin plate from one of the cupboards.

"This is fun!" he shouted. "Now, boys,

"MEIN GOTT, WHO VAS YOU?"

soon as breakfast's over we'll go through the whole concern."

Beginning at dawn, as he had done, he had really eaten a very early breakfast, and it was just in the beginning of the morning when he and Roland and Gyp stood before the door of the after-cabin, ready to go in. As is often the case, all the after part of the Dantzic was separated from the forward part by strong partitions. There could have been a great deal of water in one section of her and not any in another by keeping the doors closed.

Ned did not have to open this door. Just as he was putting out his hand, the knob turned without his touching it. He shrank back, startled a little; but Roland uttered a loud, expectant "Woof," and Gyp sprang to Ned's shoulders. Open came the door with a quick jerk, and a loud, deep voice exclaimed:

"Mine Gott! Who vas you? Noting but a boy ant a tog ant a monkey! Better dan dose cowartly mutineers, vot leave de ship vis only their olt captain to handle her. Goot-morning, boy. I go on deck to make an observation."

"Don't you want some breakfast?" inquired

Ned. "I made some coffee, and there are fresh fish."

"Thank you," said the captain. "I will try dose fish, but there vas cold vittle enough in de cabin to last me a veek. You come aboard in de night? Goot!"

Ned rapidly told the story of the broken oar and his later adventures. While doing so, his eyes wandered all over the captain. He was a large, strong-looking man, in a handsome blue uniform, with a face that looked as if its owner was not likely to give up anything; for instance, a steamer that was not actually going down. He listened attentively while Ned was speaking, but at the end of it he turned back into the cabin and went into a stateroom. When he came back he no longer carried a quadrant, which had been in his hand when he opened the door.

"I took an observation yesterday," he said. "I haf no need again. I know vare I am. De ship is safe, ant ve get to port onless a big storm come. My boy, my name is Fritz Rhinelander, ant I am glad I haf anoder crew. De olt crew mutiny after de gale, und dey go away in dose boat. Oh, de dog! I vas so mad vis dose mutineer I forgot de dog. Dot

94

monkey haf sense. He run up to de top of de mast ven dey try to get him. He know better dan mutiny."

He told Ned a number of other things as they now walked along the cabin. The middle of this was occupied by a long dinner-table, on which were scattered dishes and remnants of eatables. Ned was staring at these at the moment when Roland uttered the loudest "woof" he had yet been capable of, while Gyp sprang upon the table and got behind a tall metal water-pitcher, chattering vehemently.

"What's this, captain?" inquired a mellow but very matter-of-fact kind of voice, adding, "I slept like a top. She rolls beautifully. Was he stowed away?"

He evidently referred to Ned, and the captain's explanation did not make him change a muscle of his very intelligent, inquisitive face. He came forward and offered his hand to Ned; but Gyp refused to come near him, while Roland at once lifted a paw as to an old acquaintance.

"Come to breakfast," said Captain Rhinelander. "Ve haf to cook fish. My boy, it is nobody but dot Earl of Wallingfort. He is a big English fellow dot sail vis me to haf

95

a steamer all to himself. He ant de monkey did not mutiny.''

''Ned,'' said the Englishman, ''I am now the cook of this concern. We will adjourn to the caboose. I am the only man living that really can cook fish and make coffee.''

Just then a roll of the vessel made him sit down in a chair, but he did not lose his dignity. He only stroked his long, red beard and mustache for a moment, and then he arose, remarking to Ned:

''Boy, you must call me Mr. Wallingford. Bring me a fish.''

''Are you the Earl of Wallingford?'' asked Ned, somewhat bluntly.

''That's when I'm in England or among European savages,'' replied his lordship, gravely. ''Not when I am drowning upon this sort of steamer. Do you think we shall float all day, captain?''

''Not so long as dat,'' said the captain. ''You drown pretty soon. I am so glad ve are vell insured. Come along.''

''Were there no other passengers?'' asked Ned. ''Is she sinking?''

''He is all ve haf,'' responded the captain. ''He is enough ant a leetle more. If de ship sink it is because he is on board. No, dere is no harm. She is all cargo. If water is in de hold, I care not. All dot cargo is barrels, ant dey keep out de vater. All de staterooms is cargo. It is so vis de cabins on deck. Dot deck cargo is spoil, but it is insured. Nobody lose money by dis voyage—except dose mutineer. I make dem pay for de boats onless dey all get drown. My Lort! I vant my fish right avay.''

On went the queer earl and the comical old German navigator, and Ned followed them with Gyp on his shoulders.

"I've had my breakfast," said Ned. "I'll just look around the ship."

"No," said the earl, "I want you to come along and explain how you left America and how you boarded this very lucky ocean tramp. Come and talk while I'm cooking. I tried to cook that monkey yesterday, but he got away and went up the foremast. Took my other hat with him, too, and spun it away to leeward. He is a very fine monkey."

Somewhere or other Ned had heard of steamships called "ocean tramps," that went everywhere, and he felt more and more curious about the strange craft upon which he had

97

landed. He put in questions about her every now and then, while he was explaining his own voyage, and he learned a great deal. He found, for instance, that Roland's owner was already in New York, and that Gyp had been a pet of the ship's mate, now at sea in a boat with the rest of the crew. It was three days since they rowed away, in spite of the commands of Captain Rhinelander, and nothing more could be said about them. Moreover, Ned felt that it was a very remarkable thing to be at sea in a tramp steamship, with an English earl, a dog, a monkey, and a German captain. He said to himself:

"I'm going to hunt around and see if anybody else was left on board. I'm going to find some new oars for the Whistler, too. If it hadn't been for that other oar breaking in two, I'd never have been here. Hear that dog bark! He's found something!"

CHAPTER III

The westerly wind which had carried Ned away from land had blown itself out, and another kind of wind had come in its place. Captain Rhinelander remarked to his lordship, the Earl of Wallingford, the cook of the Dantzic:

"It vill be a nor'easter, but it vill take us in de vay you vant to go."

That was before Roland's fit of loud barking began, and the earl replied:

"I must go and ask the monkey what that is. He is all the lookout on deck."

He had been, but Ned was there now, standing face to face with another boy of about his own age, who had inquired:

"Who on earth are you? There wasn't any such fellow on board."

"Came aboard in my own boat," said Ned. "I thought everybody was gone but the cap-

99

tain and Mr. Wallingford. Who are you?
Where'd you come from?''

"Came from Boston," said the newcomer.
"I'm Sam Pickering. I saw your boat."

"Boston? Why, I came from just beyond
Salem—that is, my boat did. I'm from Chicago. How did you get here from Boston?"
asked Ned, with a feeling that his eyes were
widening.

"I got on at Hamburg," said Sam, coolly.
"I went over there as cabin-boy in a ship that
was sold when we got there. I couldn't get a
new place on any ship for America, so I came
aboard the Dantzic as a stowaway. Kept hid,
you know."

"Didn't you kind o' starve?" was the next
idea uttered by Ned.

"Guess not," said Sam. "I had a little
money, and I bought things of the crew. But
I was away below when they left the ship.
The captain doesn't know I'm here now—"

"Yes, he does," growled the deep voice of
Captain Rhinelander behind him, and the mellow tones of the earl added:

"Stowaway? I think I would like to cook
a stowaway. Better than any monkey."

"No," said the captain; "ve make some

crew of him. Sam, vas any more stowaways down in dot holt?"

"Not another one that I know of," replied Sam, "but Ned and I can scout around and find out. I've been up and about every day since the storm, specially at night. I saw him h'ist his boat on board, but I reckoned it was a pretty big man that did it. He isn't any bigger'n I am."

"There wasn't anybody with me," said Ned.

"I know there wasn't," replied Sam. "Captain, I guess I can work my passage the rest of the way. You're short of hands now."

"No," said Captain Rhinelander, "ve haf all de crew ve need, onless it vas anoder monkey; but I vill put you ashore ven ve get there. Dot Englishman, he vos de passenger, ant now he is de cook. You take his place ant be de passenger."

Sam had been in some doubt as to his reception by the captain. He had not been afraid of Ned, however, and he had come out of his hiding-place intending only to speak to a boy.

"I shall have one more to cook for," remarked the Earl of Wallingford. "I am glad of that. I hope he is a good eater. Ned, you and he go a-hunting. I don't believe we any of us know what there is in this ship. Hunt awhile, then come back and wash dishes."

"I vill take a glass on de upper deck, ant be de lookout," said the captain, and away he went, but the cook, the earl, remained.

"I did intend going back to my books," he said, "but this is too interesting. I will go aft now, and see what exercise I can get out of that wheel. This boat needs steering badly."

So she did, and he proceeded to do all he could for her rudder, with instructions from the captain. But she was not going fast enough to make the direction in which she sailed of any great account.

The forenoon had set in remarkably on board the Dantzic, and all her crew were busy, including Gyp, who had gone up the mast to just above the place where fluttered out the flag of the free city of Hamburg upside down, as a signal of distress. Perhaps it was his duty to watch that flag.

On shore Mrs. Tompkins had deemed it her duty to pay another visit to the boathouse and its keeper, and she went in an anxious state of mind concerning her boarder.

"Yessum," had been the equally anxious reply of Mr. Lancashire, "I'm greatly in fear that I've lost that boat. 'E was not so good a boatman as I thought, ma'am. Belike 'e vent out too far. Young fellers is very wentersome. I'm afeared o' the vurst, ma'am."

"It's dreadful!" exclaimed Mrs. Tompkins. "What will his folks say? Who cares for your old boat! You ought never to have let him go out in it."

"I keeps boats for 'ire, ma'am," he rejoined, indignantly. "I never 'ad a man drowned from a boat o' mine to this day. Them as upset always got ashore. That boat o' his'n'll drift in, and ve'll know about it then."

She was in a peck of trouble, and did not know exactly what to do about it.

So were not Ned and Sam, however. The whole affair of the Dantzic seemed to grow brighter to both of them, now that each had another boy for company. As for Roland, he appeared to get the idea that he and his two friends were hunting for somebody, and it was his very nature to hunt.

"It's my first follow - my - leader on a steamer," said Ned. "I don't know anything about it."

"There are heaps to know," replied Sam. "I don't begin to know where things are. Let's go down into the engine-room."

Down they went, taking lanterns with them, but it was the gloomiest kind of place after they got there. No fires in the furnaces; no steam in the boilers; no motion in all the tremendous machinery.

"All as dead as a herring," said Sam. "It'd take a lot o' men to get her a-going again. But the captain's wrong about one thing."

"What's that?" asked Ned.

"Why," said his new friend, seriously, "there is a leak—big one. I heard the captain tell that English feller there wasn't—"

"He's a lord," interrupted Ned. "He's the Earl of Wallingford."

"Don't care if he is," replied Sam. "Guess he'd drown if she went under. The captain said there wasn't much of a leak, but there is. That's what scared the crew. It's gaining steady, whether he knows it or not—"

"And all the boat we've got is the Whistler!" exclaimed Ned.

"Tell you what," shouted Sam, "we can get her ready. Come on to the spar and sail room. We can fit her out for a cat-boat, so we won't have to row."

"That's the thing!" said Ned. "I'd never have been here at all if it hadn't been that one of my oars broke. There was a crack in it somehow, for I wasn't pulling so very hard."

"Woof!" said Roland at that moment. "Ur-r-r, woo-oof!"

He stood still with his head and tail up, listening, but for a moment neither Sam nor Ned could guess what for.

"Hark!" exclaimed Sam. "I know. It's just as the men said. Hold your ear down here. It's the wash of the water in the hold when she pitches."

"Then it's rising?" asked Ned.

"Guess it isn't coming in any faster," said Sam, "but they shut up the doors of the coal-bunkers, watertight. That's why there's no water in the engine-room. We've got to hurry!"

Away they went toward the spar and sail room, but during all that time there had been a consultation on deck. The captain came aft, and took his turn at the wheel, with a stubborn, unyielding look on his face.

"I vill run dis ship into some port," he

growled, between his set teeth. "If dose cowartly mutineers had not let de fires go out, ve would haf been dere now!"

"Right," said his lordship, cheerfully, "and they are all drowned by this time. Our turn'll come by about six o'clock to-night, I should say."

"No, it won't," said the sturdy German sailor. "Not if dis vint holts goot."

There was much more to be said, but at the end of it the English earl strolled away to the cook-room.

There was, therefore, nobody but Gyp and Roland to watch the boys when they came up from below and went to the Whistler, so loaded that they could hardly walk. Working together they were able to swing the boat in and land her on the deck.

"In with the mast now," said Sam. "We couldn't set it up after getting into the water —not half so well. Now the boom and sail. Four pair of oars. Anchor. Lots o' rope. Fishing-tackle. They call those little water-barrels barricoons. Hold all we'll want."

"Big job now," said Ned, "if all those slabs of lead are to go in."

"If you don't ballast her you can't sail

her," replied Sam. "I know about boats. Used to live on Nantucket. The fishermen'll go almost anywhere in a boat like that, but you've got to know how. We'll have crew enough, too."

The Whistler was by no means small, as Ned had found to his cost when he tried to row her, even with two oars, for her full allowance was three pairs, and she now had a spare pair, "in case one of 'em broke," said Ned.

The moment the mast and sail were in Roland got in and laid down, while Gyp sprang back with the young mariners, as if he, too, meant to carry lead. They had to go again and again, but when they came back to the boat the third time, there was Gyp.

"India-rubber bag!" exclaimed Ned. "I saw that in the captain's cabin. I must ask him about it."

"Dot monkey!" sounded at that moment behind them. "Did he tell you to vit up de boat? Vell, he know a goot deal. Ve may need some boat. Ve run de steamer as far as ve can. Mebbe run her ashore. Who know?"

He did not take away the bag, however. He only shoved it tightly away, up under the forward seat. Beyond the mast he fitted in some pieces of board, so as to make a small deck, and under this he stowed away quite a number of things without giving any explanation. They were still busy when the loud clank of a hand-bell from below rang in their ears.

"Dot's de cook!" said the captain. "Ve haf dinner. De steamer is lower in de vater dan she vas."

"Sinking right along," whispered Sam to Ned. "Ain't I glad we have a boat."

Ned looked back at the Whistler, and then out at the whitecaps that the nor'east wind was playing with. He did not say anything, but his pretty, lapstreaked wherry looked like a small affair to contend with an ocean which had so completely used up the giant Dantzic.

The cook, the earl, was waiting for them in the dining-room. He wore a spotless white apron and a swallow-tail coat, but there was not the slightest sign of a smile on his face.

"He vas a goot cook," remarked Captain Rhinelander, a few minutes after they sat down, "but he know not much. He is nottings but an Englishman. He is to be drown at six o'clock."

They were a wonderfully cool, brave pair of

men, and Sam and Ned tried hard to imitate them. It was plain from what they said that the Dantzic had been nearing the end of her voyage when the hurricane struck her, sending her northward. The course she was now taking was landward. But, as the Earl of Wallingford quietly remarked:

"Certainly. But the next land she'll touch has about a mile deep of water on it. Atlantic dock, you know."

"Vell," replied the captain, "she vas all insure. So is de cargo. Vas your life insure?"

"No," said the earl. "I shall wear a life-preserver. Ned, were you ever an Eskimo? I'm going to turn the Whistler into a kayak."

"I guess I know what that is," replied Ned. "I've seen pictures of 'em."

"Tarpaulins!" exclaimed Sam. "That's what the Nantucket fishermen use. Put 'em all around and tuck 'em in."

"Goot!" said Captain Rhinelander, rising from the table. "I go all over de ship now myself. Boys, dot cook ant I vill put some more ballast in de boat. Joost so goot as lead. You go about your beesness."

"Anything heavy will do," said the Englishman. "Some things are worth more to the pound than lead is."

Away went Sam and Ned, hardly knowing what to do next, but Roland did not go with them. He had taken his position as guardian of the Whistler, and no coaxing could get him to leave her. As for Gyp, that very intelligent monkey ate a good dinner, keeping all the while beyond the reach of the earl, as if he distrusted his lordship.

After that nobody knew or cared what he might be doing, but the very first time the captain and his friend reached the side of the Whistler, carrying what the earl called the new ballast, they broke into a roar of fun.

"Dot monkey!" shouted the captain.

"'Pon my soul, he understood what I said about it," remarked the earl. "He's done it! I declare!"

Gyp chattered loudly and pointed at a row of curiosities ranged along the deck.

Spoons were in a large majority. After them came knives and forks, plates, cups, saucers, and with them almost anything that so small a man could lift and carry.

"Gyp," said the earl, "you're a trump!"

"He vas not a mutineer," added the captain.

"He stay by de ship so long as she float. If dose cowarts had been as prave as dot monkey, ve vas all safe in port by dis time."

The captain believed, and he said so, that he had done his official duty of inspecting all parts of the steamer before leaving her. He had also removed into the Whistler as many articles of value as she could safely carry. Among these, on the bottom, in place of the slabs of lead, were a number of heavy bags that went down with a chink.

Ned and Sam had followed the example of the captain, so far as a general inspection was concerned, and they were in the forecastle when Ned remarked:

"You're a reg'lar built seaman, Sam."

"Guess I am," said Sam. "Born along shore. Brought up for a sailor. Been on half a dozen steamers, big and little. Hullo, Ned! Come on! We must see the captain right away!"

Ned followed on a run, but the moment Sam came near enough to the two men, who were just then standing by the Whistler, he shouted, excitedly:

"Captain, the worst strain was above the old water-line. She's sunk to it now, and it's just a-pouring into the forward compartment. She's filling fast!''

"I know it," said Captain Rhinelander, steadily. "My lort, there is now joost about time. Dake dot oder vindlass. Put in your strength."

They were strong men, but the Whistler was now heavy, and it tested their muscles severely to swing her off, aided by the boys, and lower her into the water. Sam knew what to do, and he went with her, to fend her off from the ship's side with a spikepole.

"Now, Ned," said the captain, and down went Ned, but with Gyp on his shoulders.

Roland was there already, and in a moment more the earl was there putting up the sail, with Sam at the tiller. The water danced roughly around them, but the Whistler was doing pretty well for a boat of her size. There was a moment of peril—great peril— when she was allowed to come near the side of the Dantzic for the captain.

"Vait till she roll!" he shouted. "Now! My lort! Here I am! Shove! Out vis dot sail! Ve go! Goot-by, olt Dantzic!"

Already the forward part of the steamer was visibly lowering, and she did not roll so much,

THEY WATCHED THE STEAMER GO DOWN.

but some of the heavier seas went over her. It was not a moment for sight-seeing, however, for the captain and the earl were busy with tarpaulins. They had made a beginning when the boat was on the steamer's deck. Now, as Sam had expected, they tucked and fastened the waterproofs all around, so that as little water as possible should be shipped, and the usefulness of it could be seen at once.

"Glad we haven't got to row," said Ned. "We couldn't be kayakers then."

Away went the Whistler, but the captain shouted:

"Ve tack now, my lort. It is my duty to see dot Dantzic go down."

"Of course it is," replied the earl. "I wouldn't miss it for anything. I've been all over this world, and I never before had a chance to see a ship sink. Been wrecked, too."

The boys were silent, for there was something awful in it. She was going down fast now, for the water had many places through which it could get in. Faster—faster—then, as the great surges poured into the cabin, there was a groaning, roaring sound, as loud as a small cannon. The steamer pitched forward down the slope of a wave into the next wave; it was a tremendous plunge, and she did not come up again—she had disappeared forever.

CHAPTER IV

THE CRUISE IN THE DARK

"Mr. Lancashire, has anything been heard of that boy?" asked Mrs. Tompkins of the boathouse keeper, a little after sunset the next day. "I want to know what's become of him."

"No, ma'am," he replied, in a very melancholy tone. "If that boat has drifted ashore, it's away along the coast. I've asked heverybody that came in. Most likely 'e was upset."

"Drowned!" almost screamed Mrs. Tompkins. "This is dreadful! I never before had a boarder of mine drowned. I must find where his folks live and telegraph 'em. But his trunk is locked. I don't know their address—"

"Don't be in a 'urry, ma'am," said Mr. Lancashire. "There's more fishing-boats to come in. I 'ope 'e may get into port, and if 'e does ve'll know by to-morrer, I'm thinking."

"Oh, I can't wait!" she exclaimed. "But I s'pose I must. Anyhow, if I can get his trunk open I'll find where I'm to send word to. If a son of mine had been drowned, I'd want to know."

Something of that sort was in Ned's own mind as the buoyant little Whistler struggled on over the billows, but his way of putting it was:

"Well, I'm awful glad they don't know. I'm not drowned yet."

"First ship I ever lost," came from Captain Rhinelander, half angrily, at that moment. "But I did not lose her. It vas all de fault of dose cowartly mutineer. Ve could haf keep de pumps a-going if dey had not run avay ant let de engine fire go out."

That was precisely the reason why the Dantzic was not now afloat, and the captain was not at all to blame.

"Anyhow," he said, "I am glad I haf not more passenger. My lort, vas you de passenger now, or vas you de cook of de Vistler? All de rest is crew."

"No," replied the earl, "I'm nothing but cargo. I think the dog and the monkey are the passengers."

"Woof!" sounded loudly from under the tarpaulins, and the exclamation of Roland was followed by a shrill scream and a storm of chattering from Gyp.

"What on earth is it?" asked Ned, but Gyp was clinging closely in his lap, trying to hide his head under Ned's coat, and Roland himself retreated by Sam at the tiller, and then shoved his hairy head out as if frightened.

"Golly!" burst from Sam.

"Port!" shouted Captain Rhinelander to the steersman. "Vat he do it for? Pless my soul! Nobody but dot Englishman touch off some music joost now."

It was pretty good music, too, and it seemed to come from the bottom of the boat, the gayest kind of waltzing tune with variations.

"Just for company," remarked the earl, listening with evident pleasure. "That is really one of the finest instruments. It cost me two hundred pounds. Of course, I was cheated——"

"Music-box!" exclaimed Ned. "I thought I heard it this morning on board the Dantzic, but I wasn't sure. Must be a big one."

"Woof!" roared Roland, but the monkey chippered sadly in his place of hiding, and the voices of the wind and the sea seemed to be growing louder.

"Biggest thing I ever heard of," remarked Sam Pickering to himself, "and I've crossed the ocean three times."

It was getting dark. All that part of the ocean was exceedingly gloomy. The wind was really nothing more than a stiff breeze, but it raised large waves for such a craft as the Whistler. None of them actually went over her, but the caps and flyers of foaming salt-water which dashed along her gunwales would have sent in enough to make trouble if it had not been for the tightly-fastened tarpaulins.

The captain now crept cautiously to the stern and took the tiller, leaving the management of the sail to the Earl of Wallingford.

The latter seemed to know exactly what to do, now and then making remarks concerning yachts that he had owned or sailed, and declaring:

"I ll say of the Yankees that they know how to build boats, but we'll beat 'em yet, if we keep on trying. I'm not sure whether this thing is going for the Queen's cup or for Davy Jones' locker."

There had been plenty of material in the

storeroom of the Dantzic with which to fit out a boat, of course, and Sam had made pretty good selections, but the Whistler had all the sail she could carry, even with two reefs in it.

"I hope it vill not cloud up," said the captain. "If I cannot see de stars, I can nefer find de lant."

"Woof!" responded Roland, but what he referred to was the fact that the music-box had played out its waltz, and there was no more racket coming up from the bottom of the boat.

"I think we will have some supper," said the earl. "We had to begin to get away just as I was getting ready to ring the bell. I left a fine pudding on the range, and it went down with the steamer."

"There vill be no supper on de bottom of de sea," responded the captain, "but I vill eat all you can gif me, now dot music vas stop."

The earl, the cook, had taken good care for the refreshment of the crew and cargo and passengers of the Whistler, but it was a curious kind of picnic. The wind, the waves and the conduct of the boat itself had to be watched unceasingly, and more than once it seemed as if the sea was about to take down the entire outfit at one mouthful.

"If they should make just one mistake," thought Ned, "Mr. Lancashire would lose his boat, and our folks never would know what had become of me. We're going pretty fast, though."

They were doing very well, if they were going in the right direction, but now the clouds the captain had dreaded did come. There were no longer any stars to be seen, and he was compelled to announce to his crew:

"Dey vas all gone, my boys. All I can do is to steer by de vint, so ve roll not ofer, until daylight come."

"Ur-r, woof!" replied Roland, but the monkey was asleep, and so was Sam.

Ned could not go to sleep, and hour after hour went by, while he peered wearily out into the terrible darkness that surrounded the Whistler. She was struggling bravely onward through it, no one on board of her knew whither.

"Captain!" sang out the earl. "A light on the starboard bow."

"Aye, aye!" responded the captain, but the boat was going down into the trough between two waves, and it was not until she came up on the next crest that he could add:

"More dan von light! She is likely to be a steamer. I try for her, but I think she go by. She is too far. What you do?"

"Bless my soul, I forgot it!" said the earl. "What was I thinking of all this while? I put in plenty of lanterns."

He was now lighting them as rapidly as he could. Before long one with a red tinge was at the mast-head, swaying hither and thither with the motion of the boat. Another was firmly fastened at the prow, but its color was green. A white light glimmered at the foot of the mast, and Roland barked at it in a way to suggest that his tail was wagging.

"Dot is goot!" exclaimed the captain. "I vish I knew vedder dot steamer vas going in or coming out."

"Steer for her, anyhow," responded the earl. "The wind's right for it."

"I like not to follow her across de Atlantic," said the captain. "Vell, von vay is as goot as anoder ven you know not anytings."

"If she's an ocean liner," said Sam, "she'll lead us for Boston. None of 'em stop short of there."

"Joost as likely it vas Liverpool or Havre, or de bottom of de sea," replied the captain, gloomily; but the monkey had got his head out above the tarpaulins and was chattering at the red lantern at the mast-head.

They could see each other's faces now, but it was by a mixed kind of light that made them all look melancholy.

"Seasick?" remarked the earl, inquiringly, as he glanced around from one to another. "Let's try a polka."

He reached down to the music-box, but he must have missed his aim somehow, for instead of a polka there came jingling up a grand fandango, with snatches of old song music, including a number of tunes that Sam and Ned could remember, as it went on.

"If dot steamer hear it, den she keep avay," growled the captain. "He drife me half crazy on de Dantzic. I vish de music-box vas down in her joost now."

The boys did not feel so badly about it as did either Roland, Gyp, or the captain. On the contrary, they were beginning to feel a little more cheerful with the music going and with a steamer nearing them—if she were a steamer, and if she were nearing instead of getting away.

"We are crossing her course," said the earl at last. "I can see her lights more plainly. I guess I'll let the music rest for awhile. I'm getting interested. Queerest steamer lights I ever saw."

"If that's a steamer," remarked Ned, "then there's more than one. You never saw a steamer so long——"

"Fact!" exclaimed the earl. "It must be half a mile between some of 'em. Nobody ever saw a steamer half a mile long. They are bobbing badly, too."

"Ve vill find out vot dey are," said the captain, "if de vater vill keep out of dis boat a leetle vile. I feel not so much like being drown."

The Whistler was plunging unpleasantly, and once more Roland seemed inclined to growl and bark, as if he heard something that made him uneasy.

The earl had taken note of it, and now he said to himself, aloud:

"Better ears than yours, old fellow. The wind brings it." And he added to the captain, "Why should he know enough to make a disturbance about the roar of those breakers?"

"Lant, lant!" shouted Captain Rhinelander. "If there vas breakers, there vas lant of some kind."

"Most likely America," said Sam. "It's the only land there is hereaway."

"Well, Sam," remarked Ned, "this isn't any boat to run into breakers with. In the dark, too. Surf is awful."

"Rocks!" replied Sam. "Smash us all to bits. But those lights ain't so far away as they were."

Anybody could see that now, but it was the captain himself who shortly declared, loudly:

"Four of dem. I think dey vas some leetle fishing-smack. It is two o'clock in de morning. I say ve get ashore visout dot kind of help."

"Right!" exclaimed the earl. "We can't catch 'em, anyhow. There they go on the other tack. Time for us to put about, too. Those breakers are roaring louder."

Putting about at the end of a tack was a dangerous piece of work for a small boat in such a sea, but once more it was accomplished, the Whistler going only half way over. She was still sailing on through a dense darkness, all the darker at a little distance because of her lanterns, but her crew and cargo felt better, now they had something to steer for. They were sure, moreover, that they were headed for America, not Europe, and that was a good thing to think of.

Strongly blew the wind, and on dashed the gallant little wherry, and it was Ned who shortly sang out:

"One of 'em, captain! We're going to catch that fellow!"

"Ve hail him in five minute," responded Captain Rhinelander, "but I know not vot goot it vill do. He is not so much bigger as we are."

Whatever kind of craft was under that light, the Whistler was overhauling it, but the first hail came from the stranger, in a hoarse, cracked voice, and in German.

"Pless my soul!" loudly exclaimed the captain. "Oh, dis vas de most remarkaple! My lort, dot croak vas from de t'roat of my olt mate, dot cowartly mutineer, Petrus Huyvel. Dose fellow is de boats dot get avay from de olt Dantzic!"

"Right!" said the earl, quickly, but not loudly. "Hold still. Let me answer that hail."

"Sam," whispered Ned the next moment, "he's speaking French."

"I know some," replied Sam, "but I can't make it all out. The captain can."

"Oh, dot Englishman!" growled Captain Rhinelander. "How he vas lying to dose cowartly mutineer! I vonder vil dey belief him?"

Back and forth, as the boats approached each other, went a series of questions and responses, and at the end of it the earl remarked, "How will that do, captain?"

"Vell," said the puzzled German sailor, "it vas pretty done, after all. Dey can get ashore vis daylight. None of dem is drown, but dey haf a hard time."

"Too much in a hurry," laughed the earl. "Didn't take enough to eat. 'Twon't hurt 'em. Anyhow, we're about as safe as they are. That boat's leaking and the others have been half swamped. They left us to go down with the Dantzic."

"So they did," said the captain. "Boys, vot you tink? Sometimes a boy or a monkey know a goot deal."

"Tell you what, captain," answered Ned,

"it'll be daylight in a little more than an hour. Don't let's follow 'em."

"That's what I say," added Sam. "I know all this coast like a book, soon as there's light enough to see it by."

"Port ve go, den," exclaimed the captain, "ve tack about in de dark aviles."

Another hail came from the mate's boat, but its meaning could not be made out until Ned shouted, "Hullo! We won't follow them, but they are following us."

"Right!" said the earl. "They think we are a lot of French fishermen. We are from Labrador, for all they know. They mean to try and land where we do."

"Dot is goot!" muttered the captain; "How dey vill feel like fools ven dey see me. Dot Petrus Huyvel! I vill haf him put in jail."

Ned already understood that it was a pretty serious matter for the officers and crew of a ship to disobey their captain under any circumstances. Petrus Huyvel and the rest were likely to have trouble before them. Still, what he was most disturbed about was the sound of those breakers. It seemed to come so very near every time just before the captain tacked away from it.

127

"Sunrise!" shouted Sam at last, and at that moment the music-box broke out into what sounded like "Hail Columbia" mixed with a jig.

"It is pretty goot music," chuckled the captain. "It vill sound better by daylight. There dey come, but ve are ahead of dem."

He had watched the lights of those four boats, sheering away whenever one of them came too near, and as the dawn brightened they could be seen in a kind of procession; but the nearest of them was not Petrus Huyvel's, for he had been left behind.

"The Point! The Point!" suddenly exclaimed Ned. "There's a cove behind it! That's where I set out from. The breakers are on the Point, and Mr. Lancashire's boat-house is away around at the wharf. Hurrah!"

"That's just what I was going to say," remarked the earl, calmly; but Captain Rhinelander was letting out the reefs in the sail of the Whistler, and she was going ahead like a sea-bird.

"Dose mutineer! Dey come!" shouted the captain. "Ve get there first if ve do not go under."

There seemed some peril of that, he was running the boat so recklessly, but she stood the test and went gaily around the Point, on which the breakers were dashing so furiously.

"Mrs. Tompkins," said a man on the wharf to an anxious-looking woman who stood near him, "there comes the Vistler. But 'ow did she get hup a sail?"

"That Ned Anson!" she exclaimed. "I hope he's there. I don't want to have to open his trunk to find out who he is. It would have been awful if he'd been drowned. No boarder of mine ever did get drowned, long as I've kept 'em."

That was much to the credit of her boarding-house, but neither she nor Mr. Lancashire seemed able to stand still until the sail of the Whistler went down at the landing, and one after another her crew and cargo and passengers stepped ashore.

"Why, it's a monkey!" exclaimed Mrs. Tompkins. "Ned Anson, what made you go and be gone so long?"

"One of my oars broke," began Ned, but the Earl of Wallingford interrupted him.

"It was the steamship Dantzic, madam. If that oar of his had not broken she would not have sunk. He came to save me and the monkey——"

"Dose cowartly mutineer!" broke in Captain Rhinelander. "Here dey come! Petrus Huyvel! Look at me! I am de captain of de Dantzic. You run avay ant leaf me to be drown."

Boatload after boatload the worn-out, hungry, miserable mariners were reaching the landing. Some of them could hardly walk. A crowd of shore people was gathering fast, and Mrs. Tompkins ceased asking questions of Ned in order to tell Sam first, and then the earl, that they were to come right to her house and bring the dog and the monkey. She was too late for that, however. Gyp sprang away from Ned, and in an instant he was perched upon the broad shoulders of the mate.

"Dot monkey know not so much, after all," grumbled the captain; but he spoke louder when he said, "I dell you vot, Petrus Huyvel, I vill be as goot as dot monkey. You ant dose cowartly mutineer haf lose de Dantzic! I vorgif you, but I make my report joost the same."

Petrus looked like a man who had very little to say, but Gyp chattered as if answering for him.

"Lancashire," said the earl, "bring my lug-

"I VORGIF YOU, BUT I MAKE MY REPORT JOOST THE SAME."

gage to the house. Come along, boys. Captain Rhinelander——''

"I come not now," replied the captain. "I go to telegraph the owners of the Dantzic, ant I care for dose cowartly mutineer ant de boats, den I come. Ned Anson, you ant de Vistler haf save de cook of de Dantzic ant dot dog, ant de monkey, ant old Fritz Rhinelander. Gott bless you."

"No," stammered Ned, "I'd never have been there if it hadn't been for that oar."

It was true, and it all went back to the storm, and the young ash-tree on the mountain-side in Vermont.

THE END

The First Cruiser Out

The First Cruiser Out

A Cuban War Story

CHAPTER I

ARMED AND EQUIPPED

There were brilliant lights in the great Vanderheyden mansion on Fifth Avenue. The air of the splendid rooms trembled with music, and in the larger drawing-rooms the feet of the dancers were swiftly measuring the poetry of motion.

One pair which had been waltzing had appeared to float rather than to move, and now, at a moment when the music softened and hesitated, they were balancing gracefully between two waves of sound.

The young man was tall and vigorous, with light brown hair and a somewhat bronzed complexion. The girl was perhaps two years younger, and nobody needed to be told that she was of Spanish descent. She was, therefore, a brunette beauty. At this moment, however, her finely regular features were marred by an expression of extreme bitterness —something like hatred.

"No, sir!" she exclaimed. "I have a right to speak about Cuba. I am here, among the best of friends, it is true, but I have no home. They burnt it. I am cut off from my family, from my mother. My father fell in battle with them long ago. My brothers are fighting them now. Our beautiful plantation and all around it is a blackened ruin. Our poor neighbors are dying of starvation among the reconcentrados, except such as were murdered. I do abhor these oppressors of Cuba!"

Away went the whirling movement of the waltz, at the renewed command of the music, but more than one pair of the other dancers had watched the flashing eyes and the flushed face of the speaker.

"Our stroke oar is a goner, Tom," said one young man to another. "Good thing for us that he wasn't caught before the regatta."

"She'll make a Cuban of Jack before she has done with him," was the laughing reply. "I'm almost one myself. But he used to be a pretty cool kind of fellow."

"Any fellow is cool enough till something sets him on fire," came back, as the speaker himself swung away among the waltzers.

The fair Cuban and her companion, however, were at the next moment standing still, near the entrance of the drawing-room. Before them stood a very short, thick-set man, in the dress of a sailor, and a little behind them towered the stalwart form of Mr. Vanderheyden. The latter seemed to be watching his throngs of guests, but there was a knitting of his brows and a hardening of his lips.

"Señorita," said the short man, in Spanish, "call me only Manuel now. I am almost heartbroken! We have the arms. We have the men, but we have no ship, and the spies follow us by day and night."

"But, Colonel—I mean Manuel—I have no money! No ship! O, how I long to see my mother! I shall die if I linger here!"

"Say what you will before me—" began the young man.

"You speak Spanish!" she exclaimed. "I did not know. O! we may not trust any one! What did make me forget myself!"

"You forgot, I think," said he, "that I said I would fight for Cuba. I'm a pretty good yachtsman. Perhaps I could help you to a boat of some kind.''

Around whirled the Commodore, as some men called their host, but he had put one finger to his lips and with his other hand he was beckoning.

''Jack,'' he said, in a low voice. ''Shut up! You and your friends follow me to the library. I'm a Cuban!''

''Manuel——'' she said.

''Señorita Esmeralda?''

''Come! Señor Griswold, I will soon tell you who Manuel is.''

His face and manner told something as he passed on behind them through the changing groups of the drawing-room. But for his dress he might have seemed to belong right there, and his dark, resolute face had in it an unmistakable intelligence and refinement.

''Here we are,'' said the Commodore, as they reached a somewhat dimly lighted corner of the library wing of the mansion. ''Now, Colonel Valencia, I have only one question to ask. How about a pilot and a landing?''

''I am one kind of pilot,'' returned the Colonel; ''but please continue to say Manuel——''

"I know who you are——"

"Others must not know, for I was seen in Washington by the wrong persons. I fear I was recognized at the departments and at the White House."

"You were," said the Commodore. "One of my own sons saw you. I do not know how many more. A great many people go to see the President, however. This is a free country. But your boat is ready. I own her. No slouch of a craft, either. Sails if you want them, but she is a propeller. Six hundred tons. Regular racer——"

"Thank God!" exclaimed Manuel. "But we cannot pay you."

"Pay?" laughed the Commodore. "I expect to lose her. Get your guns and men into Cuba anyhow, if you have to run her ashore and burn her."

"Commodore," interrupted the señorita, "Madame Valencia is with her husband! I will go, under her protection."

"Too great a risk, my dear girl. It is like sending you among pirates."

"If your propeller is a good one," quietly responded Manuel, "the trip is not so unsafe as it appears. No United States cruiser will stop us."

"I understand," he replied, "that the orders concerning filibusters are exceedingly strict just now, for political reasons."

Up to this moment the young man had been only an eager listener.

"Commodore," he now said, in a steady-toned, business-like way, "I have handled a steam yacht. One of the best in the whole club fleet. I'm my own master. Put me in charge, and bill me for Vera Cruz. Give me some cannon. I'll agree to land the señorita safely, but after that I want to see some fighting."

"No," said the Commodore. "Deal fair. Bring the Lincoln back to me if you can for another trip. She is too good to throw away. The Cubans need more than one cargo. Be a man of sense, Jack."

"I think I am," replied Griswold, very quietly. "And there may be fights at sea. I wish I had some torpedoes."

"Just what I can give you," replied Mr. Vanderheyden. "The new Manin tubes. The navy department will not take them. No war, you know, no use for them. I let Manin have the money to make them with, and now they are on my hands. Boat guns, of course; short range fellows; but they throw an awful pill. I'll put four of them on the Lincoln, in the hold. You can hoist and mount them after you are at sea. Will you go?"

"O, Señor Griswold!" whispered Esmeralda.

"Of course, I'll go!" came quickly back, but there was that in his eyes and manner which partly explained why such a judge of men as the Commodore should so confidently declare of him:

"You're the man. But I didn't suppose there was any enthusiasm in you."

"Made of wood, am I?" laughed Jack. "Not exactly. But I'm a good deal like my father. They say nothing ever disturbed him, but he went into the Civil War in '61, and he died at the head of his division at Cold Harbor. He fought in forty battles. I'm ready."

"Good!" said the Commodore. "Señor Manuel, push ahead. My boat will have the right sort of captain. I've known him all his life."

"I cannot express my gratitude," said

Valencia, huskily. "I was in despair. I came to see my niece to tell her so. And now by your munificence——"

"Nonsense!" broke in the old man. "I'll repeat Jack's question: 'Am I supposed to be made of wood?' In my opinion, half of us Americans are ready for war now, and the other half soon will be. I'm rich enough to indulge myself a little, without any risk at all, except a propeller that I have no use for and some guns that nobody wants. You and Jack, though, are to risk your throats——"

"I shall die when they do!" exclaimed the señorita. "I will never be captured by the Spaniards!"

"You won't be captured," said Jack. "I will answer for that. But I'm glad to have some of those Manin tubes. A pill from one of them would sicken a gunboat if it hit her."

"So it would," said the Commodore, "and a shell from the gunboat would send my bully propeller to the bottom."

"Gunners miss, sometimes," responded Jack. "I'm a pretty good shot myself. There's a war coming, sure as you live, and I'm going to be in it. According to my ideas, the United States are about as good as at war now. Spain compels us to pay for more and more navy work all the while."

Colonel Valencia's piercing black eyes were sparkling with delight and he seemed to be growing taller, but it was time for him to go. He exchanged a few hurried words with the señorita concerning her preparations, and then a servant of the house conducted him quietly to a side exit.

Hardly had he bowed himself away before Esmeralda turned excitedly to the Commodore.

"O, Mr. Vanderheyden," she exclaimed, "I cannot dance any more——"

"Dance, my dear child," he replied. "Dance, and have a good time. Don't disappoint your partners. Besides, you've a secret to keep about my boat. There goes the music again. Be a prudent young rebel, and be careful what you say."

"I will, sir," she said. "But, Jack—I mean Mr. Griswold — get all the guns you can. I don't care if we do have to fight somebody. I'd like to shoot at one of their gunboats. O, dear! It's a polka, and he isn't a good dancer. Good-bye!"

"Jack," said the Commodore, "you're in

for a great cruise. How are you on Cuban hydrography and geography?''

''Why,'' he said, ''I've been looking up that matter. Didn't know this was coming, but there's a fascination in Cuban maps nowadays. I want to know more, though. I'll go at it.''

''Go it,'' said his financial friend. ''You mustn't wreck the boat if you can help it. But I shall try and put in a seaman I know of for mate. He has been in the Cuban coast sugar and fruit trade. Knows the lagoons and inlets and currents. Good seaman, but he's a kind of devil. Hates all Spaniards, too, and they want to hang him now for something he did at Mantanzas. Killed two or three of them, I believe.''

''Fetch him along,'' said Jack. ''He may get a chance to kill some more.''

The great crush party went gayly on, and midnight came and then the small hours. One man could hardly be missed among so many, and Jack Griswold was no longer there. He was sitting in small room of a hotel, and he seemed to be assorting papers, some to burn and some to keep.

''There !'' he said, at last, ''that's my will.

I'll lock up that with the rest, for I may get knocked on the head. No, our folks needn't know till it's over. They'd make too much fuss and try to stop me. I can put in some money, too. I know something about the Lincoln. She's old, but she was built for a yacht, and she's a clipper to go. But she couldn't carry heavy guns. They say those new torpedo tubes are not very heavy. The smaller ones could be mounted on life-boats, if the life-boats were big enough. Send a torpedo shell a mile pretty well. Blow everything all to smash when it bursts. But isn't Esmeralda a pretty one! No, I'm not in love. Never was. Never mean to be. Anyhow, I'll land her safely, and I'll try to have some rifle practice on shore."

He may not have cared whether or not Esmeralda was thinking of him, but at that hour she had said good-bye to Madame Vanderheyden and was at the main entrance of the mansion, with a party of lady friends. They were waiting for a carriage, and she stepped back a little.

"It is almost too much!" she was thinking. "They are good to me, but I have been dependent upon them too long. It is a bitter thing to be so nearly alone, an exile in a foreign land. What a cold, hard sort of man Señor Griswold is! I like the Commodore better. I know I shall get there safely. I don't care! These cold-hearted Americans are good fighters, and they might fight hard for Cuba.''

CHAPTER II

It was broad noon, and yet the city had a gloomy look, for a foggy rain was wetting it, and even the best streets were out of sorts and dingy. Dingier still were the old wharves and piers on the East River, up near Corlaer's Hook. At one of these lay a trim built propeller, standing high to prove that her cargo was not yet in her. On her forward deck lounged a big fellow in a yellow waterproof, watching the arrival, along the pier, of somebody under an umbrella.

"There'll be spies," he muttered. "It's hapes o' truth they'll git out of owld Mike Donnelly."

"Hullo!" came from a wheezy voice, as the umbrella stood still near enough for a hail. "Where's this craft from?"

"From the dry dock, ye lubber!" said Mike. "What is it your business where she's from?"

147

The umbrella leaned back, and a sallow, yellowish face was exposed.

"Where's she going?" demanded its owner.

"Going to hitch here till her cargo's aboord," said Mike. "Then she's goin' to sea."

"What'll be her cargo?"

"Dhried apples and pickles, for Machias, Maine," said Mike. "Wid a deckload o' salted lumber and hay."

"You'll answer me better than that!" shouted the sallow man. "Who's her owner?"

"Commodore Nicholas Vanderheyden," said Mike. "She's to be loaded by his Pearl Street men, and ye'd betther go to them than to me for informashin. It's a good place for spies to go to — that and H—eaven."

"I'll fix you yet," said the sallow man. "I've some information already."

Mike laughed a curiously grim kind of laugh, and with it went out further suggestions or directions concerning the sallow man's final destination, but the latter had somehow a legal right to come on board, and he did so. He was not hindered in going below or in peering into state-rooms and all corners and crannies of the propeller.

"Empty as an eggshell," he muttered.

"Even her coal isn't in. We'll watch her. Sanger & Co.'ll have to give us a clean manifest of every ounce that goes on board of her. Who are you, sir?"

"One John Griswold," responded the water-proof covered party, whom he had met on coming up from the hold. "Who are you?"

"My name is Customhouse," said the sallow man. "We're going to keep an eye on this propeller."

"Do so—do so," said Jack. "In my opinion she's a suspicious character. I'd watch her if I were you."

"I don't want any chin from you," said the sallow man, in a bullying way. "You'll be looked out for, you will."

"Look here, my friend," said Jack, "you may be a customhouse or not, or anything you please, but I can take you by the heels and topple you into the drink."

"Don't do that, your honor," said Mike. "It's against the law to throw garbage into the East River. Sure, an' it's dirty enough as it is. He's a fifer."

The sallow man had been looking at Jack from hat to heels, and he did not see anything to encourage him. Yachtsman, oarsman, waltzer, society man, he might be, but he might also weigh a hundred and eighty, and there was something ugly in his face.

"I'll see you again, sir," said the sallow man. "I don't put up with any nonsense when I'm on duty."

"Hit him, Customhouse!" said Mike. "Hit him! He's nothing but a dude. Spile his face!"

"Shut your mouth!" roared the sallow man. "I'm going to report this propeller."

Away he went, down the side, and Jack turned to inquire of Mike:

"What does the fellow mean?"

"Maybe it's hush money he wants," said Mike. "His kind always begin that way. It's best not to be too rough wid them. They can make trouble."

"What's the next move?" asked Jack.

"It's the coal," said Mike. "The bunkers must be full right away. The cargo's the last thing this time. We half fill the after bunkers. Then we lie out in the stream over night and put in the rest the next day. Ye'll be on board then?"

"No," said Jack. "I'm off for New London. I'll start from there with the tug as soon as I get my telegram.''

"Things going and coming have got to be timed pretty close, your honor," said Mike. "Part o' the coal is to come onto the Lincoln from that tug, and it won't do to miss connections. We'll be out in the stream opposite the north coal yard."

"Stevens'll tend to that," said Jack.

"That's the new mate?" replied Mike. "He's been here the day. Maybe I'll like him betther than I do, but he'll bear watchin'. There's devil in him."

"So there is in me!" growled Jack. "I'm beginning to feel savage."

"I saw ye did when ye answered that spy," replied Mike. "I can whop two like Stevens meself. I'm towld ye're a hard one to stand up wid. I think you'd betther keep a hand-spike near by this trip. There'll be a queer lot, I'm thinking, if Stevens brings wid him some o' the men I saw."

"It'll be a picked crew, Mike," said Jack. "I wish you were going."

"Can't," said Mike. "I'm only a ship's keeper just now, and I don't know a worrud o' what you're up to."

"Of course not," said Jack. "I don't know any too 'much myself. We're to have an assorted cargo."

"Hapes of it," said Mike, "and I'm thinking some of it'll go off aisy when yez git it to the right market. O! but I wish I was goin' wid yez!"

There were other visitors to the Lincoln that day, and toward the close of it three men sat together in the cabin.

"Jack, man alive!" said the Commodore, "it takes time. Don't be so impatient. Even Mr. Manuel is keeping steady. You cut it for New London to-night, and have all those plows and things on board the tug. Some of them are at Noank, just above New London. Time your return trip carefully by my telegrams."

"I will," said Jack, "and I'm cooler than you think I am. But what about Stevens?"

"Spanish rope around his neck," said the Commodore. "He's insured to fidelity."

"It looks so," said the señor; "but there never was a time when the spies of Spain were busier. Our own necks would be worth very little if we were taken near the coast of Cuba. We'd never be heard of again."

"I know that," said the Commodore. "There is more than one vessel missing."

An hour later Esmeralda Gonzales stood before her dressing table with an unopened envelope in her hand.

"Writing, instead of coming?" she exclaimed. "Let me see what is in it!"

Open came the envelope, and out fell what seemed a hundred dollar greenback.

"What?" she whispered. "Money and not a line of writing? O, yes!—a scrap, pinned to the greenback."

Up she picked it, and it was but a scrap.

"From a friend. Hurrah for Cuba! Get ready speedily."

"O! How everything burns me!" she exclaimed. "To be dependent on charity! But I do need it. I can buy things for mother, too. She is all but destitute. She has some money, but she can buy nothing there. My brothers are in rags, too. I'd go ragged rather than remain here and go to parties and all that while they are suffering."

It might be even better for them also that she should remain in New York, but it seemed a kind of selfishness, more and more, as she thought of it.

"But did he send this money or did somebody else?" she said, flushing violently.
"Three of them? I would rather die! He is
almost a stranger. No, he didn't send it, but
he said he would call and tell me about the
propeller. It is too cruel to keep me in the
dark. O, dear! More cards, and I must go
down to the parlor!"

So she did, and among her callers was one
of her dancing partners of the night before.
He was an old college friend of Griswold's, and
he was an awkward fellow, for he blurted
out:

"Señorita Gonzales, Jack told me to say he
had to go out of town. Some kind of sudden
business. Something about boats, you know,
and yachting. He's a great fellow on boats."

"Thank you," she said. "I knew he was a
boating man."

"Good dancer, too," said the youth; "but
he isn't good looking, and he's a kind of iceberg. You never know just how to take
him."

"I have noticed that," she said.

Whether she had or not, she carried her
part very well in the drawing-room, and a railway train carried Jack out of the city east-

ward, but Manuel, so to call him, went to the Commodore's down town office.

"Take that," said the Commodore, handing him an open letter. "Go in yonder and read it. Things are ripening. It will only require one good push to tip over all the peace there is left, but Spain must give the push."

"I think you may trust her for that," said Manuel, but he went into the inner office with the letter.

"Heavens!" he exclaimed, as he read. "This is better than the General told me. A full third of the Senate ready for war! Almost half of the House of Representatives! What will come next? I think there will be some kind of explosion before long. I had better go out and hunt up my men and see that the guns are cased for shipment. There will be some queer furniture boxes marked for Vera Cruz."

He chatted a minute or so with the Commodore, and departed, but hardly had he gone before a gentlemanly seeming man went to the cashier's window and smilingly inquired:

"My friend who was just here, if you please. The Spaniard—I have not his full address. If you will be good enough."

"O!" said the cashier. "Manuel? He has a boarding-house in Jersey City. He is looking for employment. If you can give him a berth, let us know. Said to be a good seaman."

"Whole name, please."

"Gaspard Manuel, I think. Formerly of Toledo. He was with a Cadiz house in the Mediterranean trade."

"Thanks! Thanks!" said the polite man, but he went out into the street, muttering:

"And where did he get that saber cut on his forehead, and how came he by the ribbon of the Legion that I saw when his blouse flew open? His manners are of the quarter-deck, not the forecastle. The Commodore has remarkable visitors."

Nobody was likely to question him more than once concerning any of them, however, for some of his answers were reported as a little sudden.

Manuel went out toward the Bowery, on the east side of the city, and on and on until he turned into a side street. There, near the corner, in a basement, was a wine and beer "café," with no particular name upon the sign. Within, after entering, one could see a bar, tables, chairs, newspapers, dark-faced men playing chess, cards, dominoes, with glasses at their elbows, but it was a very unattractive place.

Through this basement room to the rear, then through a door and up a flight of stairs went Manuel, and more than half of the other men, one at a time, dropped whatever they were doing and followed him. One of them, indeed, only went as far as the foot of the stairs. Here a brawny, black-bearded man leaned lazily against the banister, looking sharply into every face that passed him.

"Caramba! No! Go back!" he hissed at this last comer. "I cut your throat. We want no spy. This is a free country."

The stranger halted, but he did not at once flinch.

"I go where I please," he said.

The bearded man turned half around and picked up what looked like a baseball club.

"Will this do, just now?" he asked. "We lay you out in the back yard. Get out!"

The stranger's eyes glittered fiercely, but he did not step forward.

"The police will attend to you," he said.

"You will not be ready to tell what hurt

you,'' said the bearded man. ''It is better for you not to be seen upstairs by some of the men. Their blood is up.''

Courage could not count in such a case. Here was the club, and above were the angry men. It was not best to argue under the circumstances, and he silently returned to the wine room.

If the men upstairs were plotters or even pirates, they were likely to be undisturbed this time.

A good-sized room was nearly full of them shortly after Manuel entered it, but there was no conversation going on. In a kind of somber silence they all waited while from man to man a sign and countersign was whispered and a hand grip given.

''All is well, señor,'' said one, and then Manuel spoke as if he were making an official report.

Faces brightened. Eyes flashed. Men turned and embraced each other. The air was full of the names of saints and divinities in earnest thanks and congratulations. There were attempts at suppression at first, but it was too much. The excitement burst forth into loud, jubilant cheering, and a waiter who rushed in was hurried out again after many bottles of wine. There was no need for concealing exultation, after all, and here was no man who would betray to Spain, or to the newspapers, or to the United States Customhouse, the cause of this rejoicing.

"We shall get everything on board soon," said Manuel, "and then for Cuba Libre!"

Hearty cheers replied to him, and there was a stamping of feet which could be heard in the room below. Here still lingered the man who had not been permitted to go up-stairs.

"Curse them!" he hoarsely whispered to what seemed a friend of his, sitting at the same small table. "Hear that? Either they have good news from Cuba, or they think they have found out how to get there. One of the Junta men came in a few minutes ago."

"I wish we had them in Havana," came angrily back. "They would all be shot before sunset, Americans and all."

"Humph!" growled the first speaker. "A good many scores of Americans have been shot for meddling with Cuba. Spain will teach the Yankee pigs another bitter lesson before long."

"It is time the United States government

should be made to know its place," said his friend. "All the cowardly republic will need is a whipping such as Spain can give her."

"She will get a sharp one!" said the growler, fiercely, twirling his black moustaches and swallowing the last of his wine. "Let us go."

CHAPTER III

On the coast of Long Island Sound, not many miles beyond the beautiful harbor of New London, there is a point of land, with a shallow cove easterly, and at the point there is a pier. Across the head of the point and on stilts of piles across the cove runs a railway track. Trains upon this track may unload at the station here provided, and whatever they so unload needs very little cartage if it is to be shipped from the pier. This is somewhat used by coasting vessels, steam and sail, but rarely by long-voyage craft. Therefore a skillful customhouse officer, not interested in watching coasters, may easily know nothing of the goings on or off here, and generally the pier has almost a lonely look.

Not with any apparent effort at secrecy, but in broad daylight, a large, strong tugboat steamed to the pier head and was moored, a score of men stepping out as her gang plank went ashore. It was high tide, and her deck was nearly level with the pier deck. On this were lines of rail, and on these rails ran a platform car. The tug had a good derrick, of course, and there was another at the railway station. Several trains may have halted there to drop the very heavy seeming goods in cases which these derricks were now set at work upon. With so many men, with steam to help, the handling was done rapidly, and all that the cars had brought was soon bestowed with care upon the tug.

"Mr. Griswold," said her captain, at the close of the day, "ready whenever you are. I haven't seen a man that seemed to have danger in him."

"All safe," said Jack. "We must be there to-morrow night, though, and our real danger will come then."

"There won't be much of it," said the tug captain. "Two steam derricks'll make short work of transferring this stuff from one deck to another. This time we had to run it on the platform car, and it doubled the time. We weren't in any hurry, either."

"We will be, then," said Jack. "Cast off. No Spanish cruisers on Long Island Sound. Every American sailor will let us alone."

"You bet!" said the captain, and away steamed his propeller with her not very suspicious cargo.

Over most of this tarpaulins were thrown, and they looked like anybody else's tarpaulins. Moreover, as the tug puffed along her leisurely course, she met an abundance of all sorts of craft, and not a soul upon any one of them saw cause for paying her especial attention.

"It would be very different," remarked Jack to the captain, "if we were in other waters, and if——"

Then he paused, but a loud laugh answered him.

"Heave ahead," said the captain. "You needn't be mealy mouthed with me. I've worked for the Commodore a dozen years. Of course, I don't know what you're up to, but I'm an American, I am. If there's going to be a war, you won't find me on any merchant steamer. Not a great while. I'll be on a gunboat or I'll be running a privateer. I don't know that any of those heavy cases came from the gun factory. I wouldn't want to know it just now; but when I want cannon for my ship I'll know how to get 'em."

"I must look out for my mouth, though," said Jack.

"Not here," said the captain. "If our men suspected a spy on board he'd have to swim for it. Once your boat's off at sea, however, there's just one danger from a traitor, and you watch out."

"What's that?" asked Jack.

"It's when you're boarded by a searching officer. Any kind of navy, you know. A spy might point out things to an enemy, or he might make a friend of yours see things he didn't want to see. Then he'd have to do duty he didn't want to do."

"What would become of the spy then?" calmly inquired Jack, looking him in the eye.

"Well!" said the captain of the tug. "If the navy officer didn't take him away right then and there, it'd be because he didn't want to ever see him again and hoped his widder'd get his life insurance money when he didn't come home."

"Ye-es," drawled Jack. "It might create a prejudice against him among the men. Might irritate some of them."

"Jesso," said the captain. "Now, let's have some supper, and then we'll calkilate how far we ought to run to-night and to-morrow to get there jest on time.''

Probably there is such a thing as being in a great hurry not to go too fast, and there was a vast amount of impatience on board that tug during many hours which followed. Some of the men could sleep. Even the captain did so, but Griswold was not quite cool enough to get into a bunk. He seemed very quiet, too, but he spent a great deal of time sitting down upon one of the cases.

''They carry a mile or over,'' he muttered. ''It's pretty short range nowadays. Those cases over there are the gun carriages. He said they mounted on pivots, to shoot in any direction. They'd do for breastworks, or they could be run on wheels for field guns. Some rifles there at the stern and forward. Ammunition. Pistols. It'll be worth something to Cuba to have this cargo come ashore safely. So must Miss Gonzales. Pretty girl. Sorry for her. She's a splendid dancer, anyhow, and she seems to have loads of courage.''

There appeared to be a great many things on his mind, and not all of them belonged to his present adventure. Among them were family affairs, college days, olden times, and a sort of general impression that his life up to this date had been of no particular use to anybody.

"There's a crowd of young Americans just like me," he thought. "Too much money, clubs, good clothes, cigars, and all that, and our lives don't amount to a pint of peanuts. I'm in for doing something. But if there's going to be a war, some of us'll go under, and from among such as keep out of the way of the bursting shells there will spring up big new names, just as there did in '61. Who knew anything about Lincoln or Grant or Farragut, and a lot of them, before the great disturbance came? It's all so, but I may get myself shot on this first trip. Guess I'll take the old man's advice, and try and bring his boat back after another cargo. Glad I've studied navigation and that sort of thing."

The next day was long and wearisome enough, but the close of it found them slowly steaming along toward Hell Gate Channel, beyond which is the East River and New York City.

"Coming on dark, Mr. Griswold," said the captain. "It'll be good and cloudy. Just the right kind o' night for our work. That's a revenue cutter, yonder, but she won't meddle with us. We're not a long-voyage craft."

Nevertheless, they were hailed by an officer of that very cutter, inquiringly.

"What have ye got?"

"Heavy iron stuff from New London," calmly replied the tug captain. "Worst kind o' deck load. Slow going."

"All right," said the officer. "Carry it in. No duty on American iron."

"Come aboard and sort it out," laughed the captain. "I'd like to see you heft some of it. It's in chunks."

No more attention was paid to them by anybody, but the darkness deepened rapidly as they went through Hell Gate.

"Now for it, Griswold," suddenly exclaimed the captain. "I saw the green and red light for a moment. They've anchored the Lincoln this side o' the coal yards. The harbor master'll be after 'em if she's in the way o' the Sound steamers."

There she lay, at all events, and she carried lanterns enough besides the green and red signals which had been shown and then withdrawn.

"Close up, boys! Throw your grapplings. That's it. All aboard! Now for work! We mustn't waste time."

"Commodore! You here?" said Griswold.

"I'm here, Jack," sang out the old gentleman, heartily. "I thought I'd be the right party to answer questions if any were asked."

"Good!" exclaimed the tug captain. "They'd let him go ahead when they might put a twist on somebody else."

It was wonderful how promptly the derricks were at work and how rapidly those cases were lifted and swung to the deck of the Lincoln. Skill and steam power are great things.

"The tug's free," shouted the captain at last. "We're off."

"Right back to New London," returned the Commodore. "Lie there till you hear from me."

At that moment Jack felt a hard gripe on his arm.

"What is it, Mike?" he whispered.

"It's where are the cases to go, sir? We came off widout Stevens. If we put them below now, they'll be covered by the first coal that shoots down from the yard bunkers in the morning."

Jack had planned all that beforehand, and so had the Commodore, but it took all the rest of the night to stow that remarkable cargo properly. With the dawn, however, the Lincoln was at the coal wharf, the delivering machinery was rigged and the coal began to come in, changing from one bunker of the Lincoln to another as soon as everything in each hiding place was lightly covered.

"Nothing but coal in 'em now, don't you see, my boy?" said the Commodore. "You'll burn up enough as you go to get down to 'em by the time you want 'em. The worst things will be the Colonel's own cases of rifles and cartridges. We're to take them in on the North River side, and we'll cover 'em with plows and furniture for Vera Cruz. There won't be any deck load this time, but the Spanish spies will report any craft from New York for Mexico and their cruisers'll be on the lookout for you."

"So will we for them," said Jack. "I'm getting into the spirit of it. We'll bring her around to the New Jersey shore as soon as the coal's in."

"All right," said the Commodore. "I'm going."

169

"Yer honor!" said Mike Donnelly. "There comes Mr. Stevens. It's a fine mate he is, wastin' his time at the other wharf this mornin'. But does he nade to know what's under the coal?"

"Not by a jug full!" exclaimed the Commodore. "I'll tell the men to keep their mouths shut, even to him. Donnelly's head is level."

"No doubt he's a good man, yer honor," said Mike; "but I don't know him yet. Would yez do me wan favor?"

"What's that, Mike?"

"Yer honor! I know it's guns! There may be fightin'. Let me go wid Captain Jack."

"Go! go!" said the Commodore. "He'll have one more man that he can trust. I'll keep your place open for you till you come back if it's a year. He's a prime good hand, Jack. He understands navigation——"

"Second mate!" replied Jack. "I've seen some of the crew! There's a good third mate, but Mike's the man for me."

"It's good wages I'm getting," said Mike, " but the old woman'll let me go, for she's wild mad about Cuba. She'd fight Spaniards wid a rollin' pin."

Stevens was on board now, and the greetings exchanged between him and the rest were hearty enough. He did not even complain of Mike's curious failure, the day before, to tell him where to find the Lincoln this morning.

"It's the second mate I'm to be," said Mike; "and the coalin' is my job o' rights. It'll all be in soon."

Stevens only nodded, and he went down into the hold. He seemed all right and sailorly, but his bronzed face was sullen and morose in its expression. He was squarely built, with broad shoulders, and he was nearly a head shorter than Griswold. He might be a dangerous man to meet in a hand-to-hand encounter, for his pale blue eyes had a perpetual threat in them.

"If he never did kill anybody," said Jack to the Commodore, "he looks as if he could pull a knife easily. He's the kind of stuff pirates are made of."

"The Spaniards would call you and all your crew pirates," laughed the Commodore, "if they caught you anywhere near Havana. You'd all be shot before the United States could interfere."

"That's the way they do," said Jack. "But I reckon we can reach the south side of the island without overhauling."

Away went the Commodore, and the elevated railroad carried him down town upon its high steel stilts.

"I must see the customhouse people," he said to himself, as he went down the stairway at the 'way-down station, near the Cotton Exchange. "The papers of the Lincoln must be all right. I told Evans to speak to the Collector."

Out he went into the street, but he saw what seemed to be an excited crowd in front of a newspaper bulletin, and he hurried forward. It did sound, as he drew nearer, as if that crowd was trying to swear in chorus, but he was tall enough to look over the shoulders of the men just in front of him and he read the huge, black, terrible lettering:

UNITED STATES CRUISER MAINE
BLOWN UP
BY A SPANISH TORPEDO AT HAVANA!
HUNDREDS OF SAILORS MURDERED!
THIS IS SPANISH REVENGE.
WAR!

"Horrible! Impossible!" shouted the old

Commodore. "I'll arm a squadron myself! I'll raise a regiment! Congress must jump! The President must act"——

"Three cheers for the old man!" called out a boy near him. "We'll all go!"

It seemed to relieve their feelings to send up an excited, furious hurrah, but a hundred throats wound up with "War! Free Cuba! Down with 'em! Blood for blood!" and other wild utterances.

CHAPTER IV

VIVA CUBA LIBRE!

"What, Commodore? Inspect your propeller to-day?" hotly inquired the angry looking gentleman across the table in the inner office of the customhouse. "What do we care now if she's loaded with guns and powder? I wish she was, sir! Torpedoes! Rifles! Shot and shell! Field batteries! Send in your manifest. Sail away. I've done with Spanish spies and contraband of war. Think of the Maine! They did it!"

"Of course they did," said the Commodore. "But you and the government and the navy must act as if they didn't until something is proved."

"O, yes! We'll act!" returned the angry official. "We'll serve Spain first-rate. We feel like it. Carry your chips and whetstones to Mexico, but you may stop and land in Havana on the way or in Porto Rico or anywhere, for all we care just now."

Out hastened the Commodore, but already the Lincoln had finished taking in her coal, all that her after bunkers could hold, and she was steaming around the seaward end of Manhattan Island to her new berth on the Jersey shore. It was a somewhat lonely looking pier, but there was a pile of cases and boxes and crates at its outer end, and against one of these leaned the sallow-faced man who at the first had spoken so unpleasantly with Mike from under his umbrella.

"She's coming here," he said. "These things are marked for Vera Cruz. I know what that means. Our cruisers must be warned to be on the watch for her, but I'm going to have another look at all that's on board of her."

Down the pier came yet another man, as if he, too, wanted a look at that miscellaneous merchandise, and behind him rolled along a heavily laden dray. He was the man who had been prevented from going upstairs at the Free Cuba café, and he was evidently under some excitement.

"Getz!" he exclaimed, hoarsely. "Have you heard the news? Read that!"

He held out a newspaper extra, and it was

as if one side of it had copied the bulletin board in letters almost as large. A fierce curse burst from the sallow man.

"We've got so many of 'em, anyway! Hope every ship in the Yankee navy may be anchored over a mine! Blow 'em all up and blow up the nation! But I believe this propeller's a pirate. We must attend to her. She's coming to the pier now, and we'll board her as she moors——"

"Will you?" said his friend. "Look behind you. We'd better go!"

Not one man, but thirty or more, and they were coming in a hurry. With them came a closed carriage with trunks and other baggage visible. The men were not silent as they walked, but rapid voices passed among them in deep, low tones, full of evil omen.

"Quick!" whispered the sallow man. "Walk along. Four of 'em have their knives out. This isn't our day. Come on!"

They heard the Spanish words for "spies" and for "death," and they did not remain to take a closer look at the arriving Lincoln. What they cared for most just then was the fact that some of the other men were restraining those two hasty fellows with the cutting tools.

"Their turn'll come," said the sallow man. "We know enough now to have her overhauled off Cuba. Not a man of 'em'll escape. We'll see her manifest at the customhouse. No matter what they swear to, that propeller's a Cuban pirate."

"Her cargo may be a good haul for our side," replied the other spy, a little out of breath with fast walking. "But there'll be short work made of her crew. The day for trifling with Yankee filibusters went by a good while ago."

They had now escaped from the pier, and no further attention seemed to be paid to them, but here came the Lincoln, slowing up, and a rope cast from her was quickly twisted around a snubbing post.

"Hold back!" shouted Stevens, the mate, at the side. "Not a man is to come on board yet. Manuel—señor—stand at the gang plank, please, and tally these fellows."

Colonel Valencia, as it was now almost safe to call him, was indeed here, but he had not come with the crowd. He was just out of the carriage, and he had turned to assist other passengers.

"Quickly, Esmeralda," he said. "Now, my dear wife. Let us hurry on board."

A thin, sprightly, middle-aged woman was she, and she seemed in exuberant spirits.

"I cannot thank the Virgin that so many brave men were killed," she said, "but this terrible affair of the Maine will bring freedom to Cuba. I wish so much to see Captain Griswold!"

"There comes the Commodore!" shouted Jack, at the gang plank. "Stevens, I'll stay here. You see to the mooring."

"No," replied Stevens; "I must examine these men. We want no traitors."

"Go!" said Jack, suddenly. "I'm captain of this ship. I don't mean to speak twice, either!"

His whole manner had changed as if by a shock of electricity, and so, for an instant, did that of the mate. But they were looking into each other's eyes, and men who mean business understand one another very easily.

"Look out for 'em, then," said Stevens. "Weed 'em out."

He turned away as he spoke, and now his face was black with rage as he shouted an oath at the man who was fastening the hawser.

To his astonishment, something quite as bitter came hurtling back, ending with:

"Mind your mouth a bit, man, when ye're spakin' to Mike Donnelly. We're not at say yet, and I might break your face in."

"I won't have any mutiny——"

"You'll have your bones bruk——"

"Silence!" came at that moment from Captain Griswold. "You two attend to your work without quarreling."

He did not swear, but the Commodore was now near enough to hear him, and he exclaimed:

"That's Jack! He's got the right stuff in him. But I shouldn't wonder if he had to shoot some of his crew."

The Colonel was now at his post, and the first man who tried to pass him was stopped peremptorily. He seemed to be a Frenchman, but, although he spoke English, he could not answer a curious question that was put to him. In vain did he explain that he had been hired by Mr. Stevens. He was ordered back upon the wharf with no other explanation than that the crew list was full and that no more men were wanted. The next man was a Mexican, and he, too, was sent ashore.

Then followed a score whose faces evidently were known, but four more who referred to the mate were promptly rejected, and Captain Griswold now turned to him, asking:

"Stevens, what does this mean?"

"The Commodore's orders, as I understood him. He needed men——"

"No such thing!" roared the old man.

"I've a dozen more of my own coming. Men I know and can bet on. We'll have the biggest crew I ever sent out in a craft of her tonnage. All right, though. I'll see the ladies to their cabin."

Their baggage had now been brought on board, and down it went.

"What very good staterooms!" they both remarked, on reaching them. "It's like a passenger steamer."

"Built for a yacht," said the Commodore. "Plenty of passengers, too, this trip. Jack'll have more than a hundred and sixty fighting men, if he should need them. Good gunners, some of them. Artillerists. He can put the señorita in command of them. I must go now. You'll have a good voyage——"

Rapid, though hearty, were the farewell remarks, and he was on deck again to call

Jack aside and tell him more about the Maine and about the feeling at the customhouse.

"I don't care how soon you turn the Lincoln into a cruiser," he said.

"Soon as we're off Key West," replied Jack. "Then it'll be a run for life and death to get around Cape San Antonio and into the Archipelago de las Cannarreos. Manuel says the arrangements for our landing on the coast are reported to be all secure."

"That's too much to say," said the Commodore. "You may find a Spanish regiment waiting for you. Look out!"

"No rashness at all events," said Jack; "but I mean to be ready to throw shell. It's all nonsense, Commodore! The United States and Spain are already at war! We have lost a cruiser and hundreds of men by treachery. They have weakened our navy, first fire. You wait till you hear from the country. Spain will deny. She will regret. But she will chuckle and get ready to hit us again. This blow is her menace and our warning."

"That's so," said the Commodore, slowly. "But how Mike and the men are rushing the goods on board. Stevens is doing first-rate, too. He's a driver."

"Ye—s," said Jack, "but I don't want any men on board that belong to him. One captain is enough."

"Make him learn that," said the old man.

"Tip-top engineers and stokers. Now, my boy, for Wall Street. Get off as soon as you can. The customhouse won't make you any trouble. Just now they feel like offering guns and ammunition."

"Good-bye," said Jack. "I'll bring the Lincoln back again safe and sound."

"If you can't," growled his friend, "be sure you bust the other fellow."

Jack turned away muttering, "That's about what I mean to do," but he also had special duties relating to the stowage of the cargo, more of which was now fast arriving in dray after dray.

Nevertheless, an inspection of affairs below shortly suggested the ideas that the Vera Cruz market called for a very miscellaneous lot of merchandise, and that the Lincoln was really not to be too heavily laden. Probably her return cargo was expected to pay for the trip, but at present it was as Mike declared to one of the crew:

"Light, is she, me b'ye? Just in good racin' trim, if we have to chase anybody."

"It's a good run we could make if we was followed," replied the sailor: "but there's them aboard that's about spilin' for a fight. I'm wan of thim, the day."

Customhouse officers did come and all things were duly inspected. Papers were completed and delivered. There was an appearance of perfect regularity. In fact, there was nothing at all suspicious about the Lincoln, unless one felt like marveling why so many Mexican Spaniards were going home all at once, or, if these were Cubans, why so many of them were going to Mexico.

After all, however, the greater number of the men on board were either Americans, like Mike Donnelly and the captain, or Englishmen. It was a picked crew, beyond a doubt, so that the Commodore was justified in saying to a confidential friend, that very evening:

"Did you ask if she'll get there, Colonel? She will, if she has to fight her way in. You'll get there yourself, before long, at the head of a division."

"God grant it!" exclaimed the Colonel. "It won't take either the army or the navy long to get ready."

CHAPTER V

"Yonder is Sandy Hook, Señora Valencia," said Captain Griswold, on the deck of the Lincoln. "We are at sea. If you will take my glass you will get a better idea of the new batteries. Some of the guns are tremendous, and more are coming."

"All this water will soon be unpleasant cruising ground for an enemy," remarked Colonel Valencia, as his wife took the binocular that Jack handed her.

He was already at work with a telescope, but Esmeralda, standing near them, was looking back at a vast white shape which had swept past them.

"One of the new cruisers," she said to herself. "There are others, larger, and battleships. How terrible would be a duel between two such leviathans! The very thunder of their guns would deafen one."

So chatted they about ships and forts, and so did every other soul on board. There was not a man of any sort, sailor or landsman, whose head was not full of war, and the impression seemed to be growing among them that the Lincoln herself was something like an unarmed privateer with a naval career before her, instead of a peaceful trader carrying mixed goods to Mexico.

Strangely enough, at this same hour, for plenty of time had been consumed in loading and coaling and in getting out of New York, here were two men in brilliant uniforms, far away, who were discussing this very propeller. They spoke in Spanish, and they stood near an embrasure from which the iron nose of a six-inch gun protruded. From that embrasure might have been had a good view of La Havana, the harbor, its other fortifications and its shipping. At one point, well up the harbor, were small vessels which carried guns and from whose spars floated the American flag. They were grouped together, and around them were other vessels and many boats. Not far away were huge warships, carrying the flags of other nations. The attention of the two brilliant men seemed to be directed to this spot, and they lowered their telescopes to make remarks.

"They will find nothing, General Blanco. We shall prove that the Maine was destroyed by internal explosion."

"There is no doubt of it, Admiral," replied the Spanish commander-in-chief; "but the Americans will be greatly excited. They will cool down, as usual, but they will bluster, and Congress may debate and all that, but they will do nothing."

"Yes, they will," responded the Admiral. "This will let loose filibustering. I have a dispatch now from one of my agents in New York, which is interesting. Read it."

The General took and read, partly aloud.

"Sailed to-day, Lincoln. Swift propeller. Hundred Cuban refugees. Colonel Valencia and family. Believed to carry military supplies. Place of landing unknown. Papers for Vera Cruz." "Admiral! You are not going to let her escape you? I want that traitor Valencia myself."

"Never fear," said the Admiral, confidently. "Another cablegram yesterday told me more than this does. I have already sent out orders to watch for her. I think she will be a total loss to her owners. As for her officers and crew, they must be shot, if only

to give these Yankee pirates a useful lesson."

"I will make short work of them if you do
not!" snapped the Captain-General of Cuba.
"We have endured enough! And now they
will charge upon us this tragedy of the Maine,
caused by the carelessness of their own gunners."

"Of course it was," somewhat sarcastically
responded the Admiral. "I wish, however,
that the explosion had taken place nearer the
middle of the ship. It appears that they had
no such magazine forward."

"O!" said the General, "they will assert
almost anything in their report, but it takes a
long time to dredge a harbor bottom for
broken iron. They can prove nothing."

"At all events," continued the Admiral,
"we must double our vigilance against filibustering expeditions, for now the United States
officers of all sorts will be inclined, more than
ever, to allow Cuban pirates to slip through
their fingers."

He was not so bad a judge of the probable
doings of other men, and he could at least
imagine what would be altogether likely under
the circumstances.

Truth to tell, there were now not any men on board the Lincoln who were not aware of some mysterious reason for using first the top coal from bunker after bunker.

"Ye'll not go too deep jist now, men," had been said by Mike Donnelly. "The coal is selected. That below is betther for burnin' at the south o' Florida. It's made for the West Injy thrade."

"All right, mate," came back to him. "It's careful o' that we'll be. It's bad for that kind o' coal to be exposed to the weather, and we'll not let light or air in onto it."

In every direction, far and near, were the white sails of ships and the trailing smoke lines of steamers. It was manifest that one propeller more or less was not likely to attract attention. Each vessel was supposed to be minding its own business, whatever that might be, but hardly upon any other could there have been a greater amount of suppressed excitement. It was sure that for this crew and for these passengers there were stirring events shortly to come, and some of these events were shortly under a sort of preparatory discipline.

In the bright light of the following morning the two women were on deck, gazing at the

188

sea and at a school of porpoises in the wake of
the steamer. Oddly enough, they seemed to
be talking over the society events of the season
in New York, and bringing up the names of
their acquaintances. Perhaps for the hour
they were almost weary of war, and were willing to think of peace.

Down in the captain's cabin, however, it
was otherwise; for here he sat, with Colonel
Valencia and another man, with a map spread
before them upon the table. Stevens was not
there, because he was in charge of the ship
just then, and Mike Donnelly was forward
among the men, talking curiously with one
after another, as if he were trying to discover
how much or how little they knew about guns
and shooting.

The third man was tall, dark-skinned, with
sharp, aquiline features and small, beady,
black eyes.

"So, Colonel," said Griswold, "Cannara
is the coast pilot you told me you would find
for us. I wish he could read."

"So do I," said Valencia; "but he will
faithfully follow verbal instructions. Not even
the escaped slaves hate the Spaniards as do
these Caribs. Their knowledge of the country

is' marvelous. They are the best guides among the mountains. Those of them who have lived among the keys and reefs and islands, like this Cannara, seem to have inherited from their ancestors more information than all the naval surveyors can obtain. They know every nook and cranny, and there is no other coast on earth with so many queer nooks and crannies. There are caverns among the rocks that would astonish you—the hiding places of the old-time pirates and buccaneers. I think some of your magazines have printed papers concerning these caves. They know the lagoons and the inlets and the passages among the islands. Now, I can play pilot in the open sea, and so can Señor Stevens——''

"Humph!" interjected Jack. "He has given me some bad advice already. One reason for being glad of Cannara is Stevens' idea of avoiding what he calls the great peril of the Florida Channel.''

"What does he advise?'' asked Valencia, with a finger upon the map.

"Going this way," said Jack. "Through the Santaren Channel, in to the Old Bahama Channel, and then on between Porto Rico and Cuba——''

"To be snatched up by gunboats——"

"——and around the whole island," continued Jack; "instead of making a bold dash past Key West, just as if we were really going to Vera Cruz. The very fact of being caught so far away from our right direction would warrant our seizure and search and ruin."

"I don't like it!" exclaimed the Colonel. "We want no more advice from him. Did he say any more?"

"Only this," said Jack, "that the Spanish armed vessels are all over in this direction, watching for filibusters, ready to nab us, while none of them would be in our way by the other passage."

"Plausible humbug!" said the Colonel. "The Porto Rico passage is sealed up. We would be a rat walking into a trap. We are in no danger at all until we get into the Gulf. There are United States gunboats there, and cruisers, too, and we might, at the most, have a chance to run under the guns of Key West, where no Spaniard dare follow us. What do you think, Cannara?"

"No think," said the Carib, quietly. "Steer boat in among many islands. Señor Valencia see Spaniards on Cuba shore."

His English was very much better than might have been expected, but he had been in New York two years, off and on, and he was said to have passed through the Cuban blockade several times. Fellows who follow the sea pick up languages rapidly, anyhow. He was now intently studying the map, which indicated not only the coasts and islands, but the mountains of the interior. He took a dry pen and passed its point quickly from one name to another among the indicated uplands, remarking:

"There, there, there, Gomez camp. Fight Weyler men there, there; kill heap Spaniards there. Cannara know all places. Yankee land cargo there. Weyler put fort on hill. Catch Yankee next time. Gomez come from mountain. Kill all in fort. Get away with cargo. Now we come. Spaniard know we come. Blanco send cavalry all along shore. Hear Cannara! Run steamer in little lagoon. Heap big tree on key. Go on shore. Put out cargo. Cavalry no good there. Cuban come, maybe Gomez; take all cargo into hills and woods in dark."

That seemed plain enough, if it could be done, but Valencia added:

"And tell Stevens our landing place is about fifty miles further on. Don't give him any idea of our signals."

"Cannara cut he throat any time old Colonel say so," remarked the Carib. "Put him overboard for shark."

"If he turns traitor, the sharks may have him!" exclaimed Jack, savagely.

The small council of war did not last much longer, and when the captain of the Lincoln went on deck he saw his first mate at the wheel. Near him stood Mike, and that patriotic American citizen was apparently drawing out Mr. Stevens upon the Spanish question. There might have been fun in hearing him, but a gloved hand was laid upon Jack's arm, and Señora Valencia said to him:

"O, señor! Esmeralda and I were talking of you. Neither of us dreamed that you would make so good a captain."

"Thank you!" said Jack, politely.

"But," she added, "we do so much wish you would get acquainted with our men. They want permission to keep a night watch of their own——"

"They may!" said Jack. "Thank you again. I'll go among them as soon as I have paid my daily respects to Señorita Gonzales. She will think me a brute!"

"No!" said the señora. "You are the captain!"

CHAPTER VI

Captain Griswold was very much absorbed in his professional duties, and he was hourly getting better ideas concerning what he could and would do with his swift propeller. Nevertheless, he was a polite young man, and not one day only, but every day as it came, he paid his respects to his lady passengers. They had no reason to complain of any lack of attention, although he was propriety itself.

"Captain," said Esmeralda, the third day out, as they walked to and fro upon the unsteady deck. "We are getting nearer — nearer——"

The roll of the propeller compelled her to catch his arm just then, and he kindly finished the sentence for her.

"Cuba?" he said. "Yes, and to the Spanish cruisers. From this point onward we must keep a sharper lookout."

"Oh, my beautiful island!" she exclaimed.

"You do not know how beautiful it is. But I learned something from you Americans."

"And what is that?" he asked.

"You all love your flag so much. I think my New York friends gave me lessons in patriotism. I am beginning to feel a strange, new affection for our own flag. It begins to mean something more than it did."

"I see," he said, a little bluntly. "I was thinking of that. I wondered whether your Cuban patriots were only insurgents against oppression, or whether they had any ideas of nationality."

"I believe they have," she responded, eagerly. "I know I have. We do not wish to be annexed to the United States. We are all Cubans, not Americans. We differ in race and in religion, most of us. We want a free republic of our own."

"That's it," he replied. "We don't want to swallow Cuba. It's too big a responsibility. Love your country, señorita. I love mine. I'm only fighting now as a fellow that hates tyranny, just as La Fayette fought for us long ago. Besides, I wasn't doing anything worth while at home, and it was time I did."

Just then Colonel Valencia came after his

niece, and as they walked away the young captain muttered:

"Curious thing for me, though. Danced with her twice. Saw the Commodore. Got a new idea into my head, and here I am. A fellow's life may change kind o' suddenly, it seems. But we haven't had an incident thus far."

That very night something came to pass which might have been called an incident if anybody had known what to call it. Mate Stevens was in charge of the deck, and the Lincoln was bowling along finely. It was pretty dark, but it seemed as if she were already hanging out lights enough. The lights of other vessels could be seen, in various directions, from time to time. But the mate passed hither and thither, appearing only to attend to the routine duties of his watch, until he stood still near the forward deck cabin. Here was a box which contained signal lanterns, and he stooped and opened it, taking out two, a red and a white.

"I believe I'll try it," he said. "That looked like the flash of inquiry. There it comes again. Guess it isn't more than a mile away."

He lighted his lanterns, and stepped forward a few paces and began to swing them, up and down, one after the other, repeating, changing.

"Flash! flash! A red flash!" he whispered. "They've seen it. Whoever it is, they know we are a filibuster carrying contraband goods. Sorry I didn't get my own men on board, but I'm sure I'm not suspected. I'd be knifed if any of those pirates knew of this. That'll do. I've replied to their flashes. They'll follow."

He put away his lanterns, and when his watch was ended he went below, feeling entirely secure about his signaling. He did not care a rush for the lubberly night watch on deck of four men at a time, which the Cuban exiles were keeping, by permission of Captain Griswold. They knew nothing of nautical affairs, and they knew that the Lincoln must show lights at night to keep her from being run into. They had seen men swing lanterns before that.

Nevertheless, one man who was loafing flat on the deck forward, as if he belonged to the Cuban watch, arose slowly and stretched himself. He was covered by a long linen duster, and he wore blue overalls and a slouch hat pulled down well in front. His eyes were hidden by glasses. He did not speak in Spanish, however, when he said, in a low, angry sounding voice:

"Got him! I don't know what it means, but there was a question and an answer. What shall I do? Why, keep still till I know the whole of it. He mustn't dream that he is detected."

He did not go below at once, but stood in the shadow of the cabin, watching until he was sure he had seen more of those flash lights, of different tints and numbers.

"I won't try to answer them," he thought, "but I'd give something to know what they mean. To think of all our lives and that beautiful girl, too, being betrayed by that devil! He'll never see New York again, I think!"

There had been growing a good deal of seafaring cordiality between him and his first mate, for Stevens was a prime sailor and did his work well.

The next morning Jack was even more hail-fellow-well-met than usual, but his best marine telescope came on deck with him. He scanned the horizon carefully but not anxiously.

"What do you see?" asked Stevens.

"Not a thing!" said Jack. "Look for yourself. We are almost alone."

"Just so," replied the mate, as he peered through the glass, fore and aft. "We are making good headway, too. I'm still in favor of the Santaren Channel."

"We are going to Vera Cruz first."

"Oh!" exclaimed Stevens. "That's an important change. I won't say but what it's a wise one. You know your orders. I'm only the mate. But what about the passengers? They won't like it."

"You wait and see," said Jack; but he walked away to meet Esmeralda and her aunt.

An hour later he stood well aft with Colonel Valencia.

"Take the glass," he said. "Look northerly. Can you see anything?"

"Line of smoke," replied the Cuban. "We have seen scores of them. What is it?"

"Spanish cruiser, big or little," said Jack. "She followed us all night. She will keep at about that distance until her opportunity comes. I think she will send others after us."

"She can't know what we are," remarked Valencia; but a voice behind him exclaimed:

"O, señor!—Jack—Captain Griswold! Are we already in danger?"

"I did not mean that you should hear, señorita," he responded. "Will you please not say any more? No one else must know. There is no danger, simply because we have our warning. I shall not try to run a knot faster because that fellow thinks he is chasing me."

"I want to fight him!" she said hotly.

"So do I," said Jack, but he was as cool as a cucumber, and he laughed as he added:

"I am not good at compliments, Señorita Gonzales, but you look splendidly when you are warlike. You will have no chance for a battle, this time, however. I do not know of any gunboat that can overhaul the Lincoln."

"Of course, we must run," she said; "but I won't let you laugh at me. You said it was right for me to be patriotic."

"It is," he replied; "but we must not take any more notice of that smoke. There is another that I am interested in, away southerly. Donnelly, tell the engineer to be ready to put on all steam for a run."

"Aye, aye, sir!" said Mike, but Jack went to the wheel-house and took the helm from the steersman.

Only three minutes later Stevens came and looked in.

"I was going to do that myself, sir," he said. "If we are hailed by a man-of-war, you might wish to give the answer."

"We shall not be hailed," said Jack.

"Oh," said Stevens. "But we ought to slow up a little. They may give us a gun."

Not a word more came from Jack, but the Lincoln sprang forward at her best gait instead of slowing.

"What'll he do?" growled Stevens, as he went forward. "He wouldn't dare disobey a summons from a cruiser?"

Running at that rate, no long time passed before the southerly hull loomed up larger, and glasses upon the Lincoln were busily inspecting it.

"Spanish man-of-war," said Colonel Valencia. "She will expect to speak us. Let us see what the captain will do."

"I hope he won't come near her!" exclaimed Esmeralda. "I don't want to see one of their men upon this deck."

"One'd have to come, ma'am," said Mike Donnelly, as he passed them, "if the captain puts us within range of her guns.

"We are within long range now," said the Colonel anxiously. "I think she is heading for us. There!"

Even as he spoke, there jumped a flash from the black side of the still distant vessel, and the boom of a gun came sullenly across the sea.

"Signal to heave to, Captain," shouted Stevens at the door of the wheel-house. "Shall I order to slow up?"

"No," said Jack. "I'm captain just now. You let things alone."

Blacker and faster rolled the smoke from the smoke-pipes of the Lincoln, and swifter still she sprang from sea to sea.

"Twenty knots is in her," thought Jack. "She is going that now. We shall not come within three miles of that fellow, but his guns'll throw shell twice that distance. We'll have to risk his gunnery."

"He's no right to make us heave to," growled Mike, as yet another gun rang out. "The captain won't mind him."

"If he did," remarked one of the Cuban passengers, "a lot of us fellows 'd suffer for it."

There might be two opinions about that. The Lincoln was not now in Spanish waters.

The right of search could be exercised legally only under certain circumstances. Experience had shown, however, that an accused vessel, apparently headed for Cuba, would probably be roughly dealt with.

The American flag should have been a protection, but now a round shot went right over the propeller, as if to convey the sternest kind of warning.

"They won't come so near again," shouted Captain Griswold. "On with her! Let 'em blaze away. We're going three knots to their two. They dare not sink us. It would be worse than the blowing up of the Maine."

Therefore, whether or not the officers of the Spaniard were astonished, or out of temper, a fourth and fifth gun were disregarded, and they were left every minute further and further astern.

"I wish," said Jack to Mate Stevens, as the distance increased toward safety, "that one of Uncle Sam's cruisers had been within sight."

"If there were," said Stevens, correctly, "the captain of her would tell you we were bound to answer the hail of a man-of-war. He'd hold you to account."

"So he might," said Jack. "He'd blow me up and tell me to go ahead. Our cruisers have heard the news by this time. The navy men 'll be as mad as so many hornets. I am!"

It was plain enough that if Stevens had been in command he would have obeyed the letter of the marine law, and not the spirit of the Cuban filibuster, but Esmeralda walked straight into the wheel house to say, with great energy:

"O! I'm so glad we beat 'em! Thank you ever so much for going ahead. I didn't seem to care if their cannon balls hit us. I wanted to shoot back."

"We will before long, señorita," said he.

CHAPTER VII

THE YANKEE CRUISER

The Spanish cruiser made but a brief show of pursuing the Lincoln. Perhaps she had other business on hand, and perhaps it was too evident that the Yankee had the heels of her.

"Slow up now," commanded Captain Jack. "We're safe."

But he was only a few miles further southward when there were two Spanish flags instead of one. A small, swift looking gunboat had arrived within hailing distance of the cruiser he had distanced, and speaking trumpets were at work.

"Filibuster with arms for the rebels. One of our men on board."

"Got away from us," was roared back. "Follow and catch her or sink her. Chase her into Spanish waters before you attack. Shoot or capture every man on board."

"Aye—aye!"

"Go ahead! Don't waste a moment."

On went the trim little gunboat. She was, of course, neither armored nor heavily armed, but she was built for speed, and she carried four long, dangerous-looking guns, quite sufficient for the destruction of any mere merchant steamer. She could have held her own in a pretty hard fight, for her class of vessels are the hornets of the sea, and Uncle Sam has a number of them, with a larger lot building.

The night came, but there was no more signaling, for Griswold himself or Mate Donnelly was all the while on deck.

When morning came, they saw again that tell-tale smoke at just about the same distance behind them.

"She's a-coming, your honor," said Mike to his captain. "We'll hear from her yet."

"We may shake her off," he replied, "but if we can't it may be bad for her."

"Hurrah!" came at that moment from the lookout forward. "Yankee cruiser! Steaming this way."

"Steer for her!" shouted Jack. "Men! not a word to her about the Spaniard. We mustn't be reported or get into the newspapers."

"All right, sir," came back from several voices, and the Lincoln sped on.

"One of your White Squadron," remarked Colonel Valencia, a little later.

"Splendid vessel!" exclaimed his wife at his side. "O! how I wish poor Cuba had a navy."

"She'll have ours working for her pretty soon, I think," said Jack.

"Captain Griswold," asked Esmeralda, "will your own people board and search you? Would they stop us?"

"No, señorita," he replied. "Our papers are all right. We are ready for a search. That is the cruiser New Hampshire. She's a perfect beauty."

So she was, to eyes that were considering her as a fighting machine, and before long she was within hail.

"Shall I bring my papers?" asked Jack of the United States officer at her larboard rail.

"No!" came sharply back. "You are reported to us by telegraph. We must send an inspector on board. Heave to!"

A boat was dropped from the side of the New Hampshire. An officer and men went down into it, and in a few minutes more the officer was on the deck of the Lincoln.

"Hullo, Jack!" he said. "Never thought of meeting you at sea till I saw the telegram. Turned pirate, eh?"

"Yes, old fellow," replied Jack. "I got as tired of dancing as you did on your Saratoga furlough. Piracy is better fun. Going to inspect cargo?"

"Thoroughly!" said the lieutenant. "If you're a blockade running filibuster we must stop you. I see lots of Spanish Mexican passengers."

"Miss Gonzales," interrupted Jack, "Señora Valencia, Colonel Valencia, permit me to introduce my old friend, Lieutenant Adams of the New Hampshire. He is about to arrest you."

Exceedingly ceremonious were the responses, but the lieutenant's eyes were twinkling as he hastened to the further performance of his duties.

"Got you now, Jack!" he said. "You've a first-rate reason for being a Cuban. Under the command of Colonel Gonzales—was that her name? Fine officer. Looks terribly courageous. Come on, now. Show me your arms and ammunition."

"Find 'em," said Jack. "Look anywhere you please."

The lieutenant did seem to look, but at last he declared:

"Papers are all right. Cargo O. K. I won't disturb your crates of furniture. Plows and harrows are just the thing. But, my boy, run well into the Gulf after you pass Key West, before you turn east again. There are gunboats and revenue cutters cruising all the way from Havana to Cape San Antonio. Pass the cape in the night. Don't say any more. All of us fellows have heard from the Maine. If you have to fight—fight!"

"We are a peaceful, unprotected merchant steamer," said Jack.

"Of course you are," snapped Adams. "With as peaceful a lot of Quakers on board as I ever saw. No guns. No ammunition. No arms of any kind. But you'd better buy some and mount them as soon as you are out of the Florida Channel. My report of this inspection will pass you with any of our fleet. Use tarpaulins, you know. I haven't seen anything suspicious."

Up the companionway he went, and Jack followed him; but the waggish lieutenant strode straight toward the lady passengers.

"Madame!" he exclaimed, "Captain Griswold is young and rash! I beg that you will keep him out of danger! Señorita Gonzales, I trust that you will arrive safely in—in—in Vera Cruz. I didn't know that there was a landing place of that name in—in—well, in Mexico. But Mexico is such a large island.''

''It is, indeed,'' said Señora Valencia. ''We will take good care of Jack. But don't you think your own ships of war need to be taken better care of? Torpedoes are bad for them.''

His eyes were flashing angrily as he responded:

''Thank you for that, madame! All the care we want just now is the open sea and a Spaniard in fair range, and the right to fight her. We will remember the Maine!''

''I'm afraid I'm revengeful,'' said Esmeralda. ''I should wonder if you were not angry—all of you. It was a cowardly murder. I must not say too much.''

''Don't say anything, I beg of you,'' he interrupted. ''If there is anything I ought not to know, I do not wish to know it. Duty is duty, and I am not bound to report any mere guesses.''

He ended with a low bow, and turned away

quickly, as if he were afraid she might tell him something perilous. Down he went into his boat, and hardly another word was exchanged between him and Jack. The latter did not see or hear his friend when he made his report to the captain of the New Hampshire, but that distinguished officer listened with stolid calmness to the very end.

"Adams," he then said, "the señorita is contraband of war. So is Griswold. So are Colonel Valencia and his wife. They are very plain reading as to the destination of the Lincoln. You saw nothing?"

"Not one thing," said the lieutenant. "All just as it should be."

"Glad of it," said the captain. "But now I am sure about that, where have they put the guns and carriages?"

"Under the coal," replied Adams. "The other stuff is in the furniture crates and under them. Covered fine!"

"All right!" exclaimed the captain. "I am glad we cannot possibly know anything about it. Let her go right along to—Vera Cruz—if that's the name of the landing. Good luck to her."

The Lincoln was already going, and for

some reason or other the tars of the New Hampshire gave her three cheers.

"It's all right, b'yes," remarked one of them, who had been with Adams. "It's me own cousin, Mike Donnelly, is mate of her. He towld me not to say a worrud, and I won't; but that there sassy little propeller is own cousin to a torpedo boat, and it's a good family to belong to."

Another cheer went up, and was loudly responded to from the Lincoln. There was a waving of hands and hats, and the official inspection had done no manner of harm. All the formalities had been complied with, at all events, and only an ill-natured person would have hinted that less had been done than might have been attempted, at least before the submarine explosion at the Havana.

"Mike," said Captain Griswold, an hour later; "we shall not be boarded again. We'll make a long run to-night. By to-morrow morning we shall be off the Dry Tortugas. It's time to begin getting out the guns. It may take days to mount them. We can do it while we are running toward the Yucatan Channel."

"We'll begin right now, sir," shouted Mike.

"Come on, men! We'll turn ourselves into a gunboat the day."

The night it was, rather, and no man on board did more, in his way, than did Mate Stevens. He was zealously determined to get things out from under the coal and up on deck. Slow, hard work it was, however, for care had to be used, owing to the motion of the vessel. Thus far the weather had been pretty good, what the sailors sometimes call Gulf Stream weather; but signs of something rougher were showing, and there was almost too much sea for the handling of heavy goods.

"Steady, Captain," said Mike, at last. "The carriages are h'isted. Let's leave the guns till it's quieter."

"I'll mount one aft before I sleep again," said Jack. "I think we have passed our cruisers in the dark, but I'm thinking of that shark of a Spanish gunboat. I hope we've thrown her off."

"No, we haven't, Mike," he said somewhat later, "The sun's almost up, and there's a smoke in the wake of us, hull down. She has hung on like a bloodhound. She mustn't come too near, after we tack easterly. To be overhauled by her then might be death."

"Captain," said Stevens, coming up, "I think we've done about enough. We couldn't use one of those tubes, even if we had it on deck."

"Couldn't we?" said Jack. "Well, Stevens, it would be ornamental. Let's have one up for a show. I'd like to see how it looks. They are finished handsomely."

Stevens made no further objection, but, as he turned away, he caught a singular expression upon the face of Colonel Valencia and another in the beady eyes of the Carib, Cannara. The hand of the latter was upon the hilt of his sheath knife.

"My God!" muttered the mate, as he went aft; "can it be possible that they suspect me? Nearly four score knives would be out if they did. I'll be careful. I won't go near a gun. If anything should happen to one of them, I'm a dead man. I'll look out for that Carib!"

CHAPTER VIII

THE FIGHT IN THE STORM

"It's almost a hurricane, Captain Gris-- wold," said Mate Stevens, a number of hours later. "You are heading southerly, right into the teeth of it."

"You're no sailor," growled Jack. "Would you have me put her broadside to this sea?"

"Safest to heave to," replied Stevens.

"You're a traitor!" hissed Jack between his teeth, but the wind prevented the mate from hearing, and he himself added:

"You might run into an enemy's hands."

"We are running away from everybody," said Jack, more loudly. "I hope that gun carriage won't break loose. We'll have more of 'em up to-morrow."

"To tell what we are," almost sneered the mate. "It's dangerous."

"They'll be dangerous enough for anybody that comes after us," said Jack. "But the next will be mounted forward, and the other two will look out at the middle cabin windows. We shall be pretty well armed, Mr. Stevens.''

The mate had no more to say, but the thought in Jack's mind was, ''The fellow is giving himself away fast enough. For us to heave to now, would only be to wait for the fellow that's following us. He is too willing to have us defenseless, but it isn't time yet to tell him what I know. I'm going to leave him to the Cubans.''

That was a pretty savage decision to make, considering the kind of Cubans he had on board.

Of course, the Lincoln was not making rapid headway, but that would also be true of any other steamer which might at that hour be facing the gale. Fiercely as this was blowing, it did not altogether prevent the engineer and a brace of mechanics from doing a good deal for the firmness of the moorings of the gun carriage. This was a pivoted affair, and upon it now rested what looked like a not very long brass cannon, breech-loading. One skilled in such matters could have judged by its apparent weight, or lack of weight, that it was not expected to bear the charges of powder demanded by long ranges. It was more of a boat-gun, but it would throw a terrible missile. It was one of the several patterns recently invented, and as yet there had been no opportunity to use any of them in actual warfare. Nobody as yet knew exactly what they could do.

"Mike," said Jack, shortly afterward, "you take the wheel for a while. I can trust you. Keep her head as it is. This gale can't last forever. I must take a watch below."

Down he went, but no watching of his was needed in that hold. Cannara the Carib sat astride of one of the as yet unmounted tubes. In every direction crouched or lay the dark-faced refugees from Spanish tyranny, their eyes glancing fiercely hither and thither. Every man of them knew that he was now steaming on into deadly peril, and somehow it had gone around among them that there was treason on board. What if some enemy of Cuba should be seeking an opportunity to spike or otherwise injure one of those splendid guns?

What if their coming should have been already so announced as to prevent them from landing? What if they were betrayed before-hand in some inscrutable manner to the swift revenges of Spain?

The very storm itself added to the gloom that surrounded their situation, and they all wore the look of desperation belonging to a struggle for life or death.

Jack spoke to them cheerfully, and went on into the cabin.

"O, Captain," exclaimed Señora Valencia. "Are we in any danger?"

"None at all!" responded Jack. "But I wish you and Miss Gonzales were more comfortable. This rolling and pitching——"

"Hark!" shouted the Colonel, springing to his feet. "What's that?"

"Sounds like a distant gun," replied Griswold. "May be a signal of distress from some vessel or other. I must go up and see about it."

"I'm coming," said the Colonel. "That was no signal gun. It was shotted."

In a moment more they were on deck, but Señora Valencia held back her niece.

"Not now," she said; "not in such a storm. You must stay here."

"But, aunt," exclaimed Esmeralda, "if there is to be fighting, I must see what is going on!"

"No! no!" said the Colonel's wife, firmly.

"Women are not wanted on deck at such a time as this. The captain would not like it."

"I'm not under his orders."

"Yes, you are! He must not be hampered in any way."

So she said, but he was feeling dreadfully hampered, even then. In spite of the driving rain and occasional drifts of fog, all eyes on deck were able to see at intervals the unsteady shape of another steamer, toiling along at little more than a mile behind them. She carried a bow gun, too, and it was this which had spoken, as if commanding the Lincoln to slow up and wait for her arrival.

"Curse it!" said Jack, angrily. "This sea! Tossing us about so! I'm afraid I couldn't hit her if I tried."

"She can't hit us," said Stevens. "Of course we are not ready for an artillery match with a gunboat. There she goes again."

"Let her blaze away!" shouted Jack. "Mr. Engineer Brady, is that gun ready?"

"I've sent down for shells," responded Brady. "That shot came too near for the fun of it. She had no right to send it."

"Send one back," said Jack, "if you're sure of the carriage moorings to stand the recoil.

It's the new recoil spring, but if it should break loose, the gun would go overboard. Do lots of damage, too."

"She'll stand it, you bet," growled the engineer. "Bear a hand, men. 'Twon't be easy work loading her. Throw open the breech-piece. Now——"

In slipped the long, slender shell, full of guncotton and fulminate, and down to its place went the breech-piece.

"I'm the gunner!" shouted Jack, and he added orders to several of the crew, who sprang forward as if they knew about what ought to be done.

"I don't know anything about the range," he muttered, discontentedly. "There comes another Spanish shell. Missed us two hundred yards. It's all guess-work and blind luck. Now! as we rise on this long surge. Steady her, Mike! Up we come. If that'll do——"

A jerk of his right hand, a tongue of fire springing from the muzzle of the tube, a thundering report, a jarring of the Lincoln from stem to stern—but all eyes were upon the Spaniard.

Her own bow gun was just speaking again, when it seemed somewhat as if it were making two reports, the second louder and more terrible than the first.

"Heavens!" exclaimed Valencia. "Your luck was good. Struck her! She isn't a gunboat, either. Only one of their saucy revenue cutters."

"She knows who we are," said Jack, "or she'd never have blazed at us in that way. We are marked for destruction."

"Guess she's pretty well marked herself," said a sailor, who was watching her with a telescope." Hit her amidships as she swung a little. Blown up!"

A third tremendous roar came to them across the gale, muffled indeed, but telling its tale as plainly as did the column of smoke and fire from which it arose. The torpedo shell had done its deadly work only too completely, and the revenue cutter was a thing of the past.

" 'Bout ship!" shouted Jack. "We may save somebody."

"To report of us afterward," savagely suggested Stevens himself. "What you have done is piracy, Captain Griswold."

"No, sir!" loudly responded Jack. "What they did was piracy. We have a perfect right to protect ourselves from a fellow that's trying to sink us."

"Captain Griswold, what is it?"

"We have beaten an enemy, Señorita Gonzales," replied Jack, very quietly. "We are not hurt, but the Spaniard is blown to pieces. We are going to see if we can save any of their crew, but she seems to have had too much powder on board, from the size of the explosion."

"O, be merciful!" she said. "Save as many as you can."

"Please go below," said Jack. "You and your aunt are drenched already."

"She wouldn't let me come, but we heard our own gun and I wouldn't stay any longer. I won't go down till I know everything."

All the Cuban refugees were now on deck, at the risk of going overboard as the propeller plunged among the rough seas, but she was about now, and was steaming before the gale instead of against it.

Only a mile to go, after that, with no revenue cutter in sight. She had gone down, of course, all that was left of her. A few fragments were seen, tossed hither and thither among the crests of foam and the dark sea hollows. The steam whistle was sounded. There were eager listeners for human voices and eager eyes watching for signs of any swimmers. But it was all in vain. Not one face or form appeared nor any voice to answer. Whoever had not been killed at once had been too much hurt or stunned for swimming. There was, therefore, no means for telling which of the many small coast cruisers of Spain had been stricken to ruin by the first shot fired in this war upon the part of the United States merchant navy.

CHAPTER IX

More fiercely blew the wind, as the Lincoln once more turned to face it, and there was no lingering upon the deck by any whose duties did not compel them to be there. The brass torpedo thrower rested firmly upon its carriage as if it did not care a cent for the terrible mischief it had made. Down below, its friends were discussing it with many expressions of strong commendation.

"Captain," said Colonel Valencia, "I don't think you could do that again."

"Not every time," replied Jack, "but the range was really short and the propeller was fairly steady on the top of that wave. There is such a thing as luck. Another shot from that Spaniard might have been ruin to us. Her gun was a heavy one for a boat of her probable size."

"If she had sunk us," returned Valencia, "my belief is that we'd never have been reported."

"That is, never heard of," said Jack. "As if we had foundered at sea. That's precisely what we must do for the Spaniard. Nobody on board need act as a newspaper man. After the war begins it might be no harm, but until then it's an unpleasant affair."

"It is, anyway," said Esmeralda. "It is dreadful! I do not like to think of it. O! how the hurricane roars."

"Not quite a hurricane, señorita," said Jack, consolingly. "I don't believe it will last long. But it keeps us from getting out our other guns. We must have about two days of hard work before we are a full-fledged man-of-war."

The two days were given him, for the wind blew itself out that night, and the next morning dawned fairly without a sail in sight.

"Jump!" shouted Jack to his men, and the Cubans needed no urging.

So many hands, so desperately in earnest, made shorter work of everything than he had expected. It was a marvel how speedily the broadside guns were in their places. The forward gun on deck was a more difficult matter, but before sunset it was ready for action. As for small arms, it was no task at all to open cases and serve out rifles and cartridges.

"Only a gunboat or a cruiser can do anything with us," was freely declared by all
hands, and the fighting spirit seemed to be
running high.

Even that one shot had made it plain that
the propeller could stand her armament very
well, but Jack remarked:

"I know something now about the effect of
guncotton when it goes off. I don't want any
shell to burst on this boat. We are no iron-
clad. Still, I think our steel sides would stand
something."

"Shot would glance from them perhaps,"
said the Colonel, "unless they struck too
squarely. That is, light shot. But those new
shells burst on striking, no matter what the
angle is. I hope we won't get hit. Where
are we now?"

"We are leaving the Gulf of Mexico," replied the young captain. "We are well south
of the point of Cuba. By to-morrow morning we shall turn northerly, and try to reach
the coast."

"Cannara!" said the Colonel. "That will
be his time."

"I shall keep the wheel myself," said Griswold, "with you at my elbow, till we are

among the Archipelago de los Cannarrios. Mr. Stevens has offered his services, but I shall then prefer the Carib. Stevens is really a good seaman.''

"Caramba!'' exclaimed the Colonel. "I suppose he is. So are other Spaniards. But we can prove nothing against him. Well, it is night now. We shall know more in the morning.''

There was not a great deal of sleeping done that night on board the Lincoln. The air was pleasantly cool. The wind was fresh. There was a nearly full and very brilliant moon. It was an ideal night for a trip across a southern sea. Nevertheless, this was a trip into the jaws of death, and the hour of the last, greatest peril was at hand. From time to time the night glasses were at work, and it was just before the dawn that Mate Stevens came to Griswold.

"Up, Captain,'' he said. "I think I see smoke to leeward. I've been keeping away from it. Have a look at it.''

Jack sprang to his feet and hurried to the wheelhouse, glancing leeward as he went. He took the wheel from the sailor who had been steering.

"The villain!" he muttered. "He was putting us right across the track of that stranger. Donnelly! All hands up and all steam on. Send Cannara to me. Call out Valencia, but don't disturb the women. Let 'em sleep."

"Aye, aye, sir!" shouted back Mike; but part of his errand could not be done. The sound of so many hurrying feet below and on deck was quite enough, and Esmeralda and her aunt were quickly on deck.

"Cuba?" exclaimed Esmeralda. "Are we nearing my beautiful island?"

"It is not in sight yet," said her uncle, peering in all directions. "What does this disturbance mean? I see nothing. I will ask Señor Griswold."

They were near enough to the wheelhouse to be heard, and an answer came at once.

"Don't ask anything, señor. It's only a smoke yonder, and we must keep away from it. We have a good distance now."

They had been going along at little more than six knots for several hours, but now the propeller was quickly called upon to show her paces.

Up came the sun, through a light haze, which at dawn had obscured the horizon, and the whole sea was clear. It was also almost quiet, and the motion of the ship was steady.

"Southerly!" shouted Stevens. "There it is, Captain. "A good three miles. We can beat her."

"All right!" replied Jack, but he was angrily thinking: "I believe it would have been less than half that if you had been at the wheel, but I can't prove it. You are a cunning fellow. As deep as a well; but there's a knife at your throat."

Cannara himself was standing near, and he did not hear that thought, of course, but he seemed to answer it.

"Señor Captain," he said, "I watch. I see smoke. I see mate tell wheelman. I see Lincoln go wrong. I know. We nearer Spaniard if you not come. Now Spaniard steer for us. Look!"

They were not exactly running away from the stranger, but were upon a course oblique to his, so that the two lines would gradually approach each other. The seamanship and speed required was to put the point of meeting of those two lines so far astern that the Lincoln would still be out of easy shot range.

She was already near enough for a heavy gun to do her an injury, but the stranger as yet showed no sign of any hostility.

"Going to steal a march on us," thought Jack. "He'll try to get a hail if he can. Stevens, see that all hands have their breakfasts. This is going to be a busy day. The men must be all right."

They grumbled at being compelled to go to their coffee, nevertheless, and the happiest men among them were the squads shortly told off to the guns and to the ammunition. The most discontented of all were the engineers and the stokers, for they were stationed where they could see and hear nothing. So they bargained with their comrades above to bring them the news as fast as any should be manufactured.

"If we are a clipper, so is she," remarked Jack, a little later. "Cannara, take the wheel. I must use my glass a little. No! Mr. Stevens. Leave it to him. I shall want you elsewhere. Nor'east by north, Cannara. Steady! Now, Stevens, what do you make of that fellow?"

"Spanish gunboat, sir," calmly responded the mate. "Our coming was known, I believe. He will recognize us. Our chances are a little thin. What do you think?"

"We're all right!" said Jack. "We must get in among the islands. We do not draw as much water as a gunboat."

"Mistake!" said Stevens. "They have some that are built for coast service. They can run in wherever you can. But the navigation is dreadfully ticklish as we near the south coast of Cuba. It's a place to run your nose on a hidden key."

"The coral reefs," said Jack, "are as bad for a Spaniard as for a Yankee. We must take our chances. Some of the islands'll be in sight before long. Hullo! A gun!"

"Nothing but a call to heave to," said Stevens. "We're not under his orders yet. Captain, I want to say one thing, once for all."

"What is it?" asked Jack.

"Don't resist until you are sunk with all hands. Pretend to surrender. Let 'em board. Then rise and take 'em. We outnumber the crew of any small gunboat. Take 'em by surprise."

"That's just what we'll do, Stevens," replied Jack, but he walked away, thinking again.

"Deep! deep! deep! He puts on an appearance of utter desperation, and it seems to cover him. Don't I know that we'd be face to face with two hundred well armed men? True, the surprise might do it, and we'd die fighting if we were beaten. I think we will trust to our heels for a while."

"Señor Griswold," said Esmeralda, as he drew nearer, "what was the danger? Is there any hope of escaping?"

"We are not in much danger yet, señorita," he said. "The enemy is half a mile further than he was at dawn."

He had gained that by changing his course so prudently; but the Spaniard was now losing nothing.

"Another shot," she said. "I didn't see where it struck."

"In our wake," said Jack. "Far enough away. I never before heard of such reckless shooting in time of peace."

"Nor I!" exclaimed Colonel Valencia. "Captain, it's plain enough. We were fully betrayed before we left New York. The Spanish naval officers all have orders to treat us as Cubans, and not at all as if we carried the United States flag."

CHAPTER X

That morning there were two cloudy-faced gentlemen in the inner office of Commodore Vanderheyden.

"Admiral," exclaimed one of them, leaning half-way across his office table, "what does Congress mean? The speeches are well enough, some of them, but when will they act?"

"My dear friend," said the gentleman in the somewhat weatherworn uniform, "be patient. I cannot tell you all that passed between me and the chairman of the House Committee on Naval Affairs, nor what I said to the Secretary of the Navy and the President. His head is entirely level and yours ought to be. You know, if you will think like a sane man, that we must spar for wind. We must engineer delays. Neither the army nor the navy is half-way ready. Our coast defenses must be put into shape or Spanish iron-clads could sail into our most important harbors. We have not ten rounds of ammunition for such guns as are ready for service, let alone the new ones. Ships are scattered. We have no transports. We want more cruisers. We must have millions of money. We must have more sailors, and an army of a hundred thousand men. Be calmer. Have you heard again from your propeller that sailed for Vera Cruz? She has not reached that port."

"Not yet!" laughed the Commodore, throwing himself back in his chair. "Yes; I've heard from her, very much as you have. You know too much, though."

"No, I don't," said the Admiral. "I have no official duty concerning her. She passed inspection, and that's all I care for. It is too late now for any further inquiry about her cargo or her destination. I hope the Spaniards won't get her."

"They may catch a Tartar——"

"Why, she isn't actually armed, is she?"

"Admiral!" exclaimed the old man, excitedly. "I'll say this much to you, as a friend, not as an officer——"

"Say it anyhow! I won't peach."

"By the time she reaches the coast of Cuba she will be a kind of gunboat!"

"Auxiliary cruiser!" shouted the Admiral. "We want scores of 'em. We will buy every good steam yacht and arm her within three weeks. How is the Lincoln armed?"

The Commodore told him.

"All short range tubes!" growled the Admiral. "She needs• one long range gun. More artillerists. More men. She wants a trained naval officer."

"Jack's a good one," said the Commodore. "I expect to hear stirring news from him before long. I'm at war, if the United States isn't."

"The United States is," said the Admiral. "Every act of preparation is an act of war. Getting a good ready is the best kind of fighting, Going in before we are ready is a loud bid for disaster. But you mustn't say any more just now. Find out all you can for me about steam yachts like the Lincoln. I must have another trial of those torpedo tubes for boat guns."

"I'll furnish Uncle Sam with another ship as soon as it's wanted," said the Commodore, "but I do wish Jack had a long range gun."

The Admiral nodded and walked out of the office, but at that very hour Mike Donnelly was remarking:

"Howly Moses, Captain! Don't I wish wan o' them things'd carry a torpedo three miles! It's awful to be shot at and not answer 'em!"

"They are nearing us a little," quietly responded Jack; "but we cannot change our course yet."

"What's that sign o' land northerly?"

"I think it's the outlying reefs of the Isle of Pines," said his captain. "The Spaniard'll have to sheer away into our wake pretty soon, or he'll run into ticklish quarters. That shot fell within a hundred yards."

"Shooting must hinder his running, I should say," remarked Colonel Valencia. "What I'm afraid of is that this cannonading may bring him help of some kind. It'd work like a signal."

"Captain!" came just then in the voice of Stevens from near the wheelhouse.

"Aye, aye, mate," and Jack went to him.

"Captain Griswold, you are responsible, not I, if we hold on under this cannonade. We have been nearly hit several times."

"Do you mean surrender?"

"No! I mean heave to and let 'em come near enough to give 'em all our torpedo pills at short range. Our four shells would do for a heavy vessel.''

''I'll think of that,'' said Jack. ''But we'll hold on a little longer. More northerly a point or so, Cannara.''

''Captain Griswold,'' exclaimed the Colonel, ''this way. A word——''

''Say on—quickly.''

''The Spaniard would not stop firing! If we slow up we are lost!''

''So is he, then.''

''He will take his chances, sir. If not killed by Spanish shell, he has a good thing of it. If we are not captured by them he is a gone case, and he knows it.''

''Not so bad as that,'' said Jack. ''I shan't hurt him. But we shall be almost within range of that fellow when we pass the Isle of Pines.''

''God help us!'' said the Colonel. ''My wife! Esmeralda! All our friends!''

''Cheer up!'' said Jack. ''We are not touched yet.''

It would have done the Colonel all sorts of good just then if he had been upon the deck of the Spaniard to hear her Captain roaring:

''Caramba! What say you? No more shell

for the long thirty-two? Only the six-pounders to work with? That is the fault of our commissary of supplies. We have wasted our ammunition."

"Never mind!" responded his next in command, with a long Spanish oath. "We must get nearer. We know who it is. We must capture that vessel."

"Sink her!"

"Not till we get her cargo and passengers," said his lieutenant. "There are pretty women on board, and rebels. Her freight is valuable. Prize money!"

"Madre di Dios, yes!" growled the captain. "I must not forget that. We shall overtake her. We gain all the while."

So they did apparently, but not by any means because they were the faster vessel. It was because both Jack and his first mate had seen something which they had not yet mentioned to anybody else. Away in the western horizon, faint and blue, was to be found by a telescope a thin line of color—the probable smoke from the pipes of a Spanish man-of-war. It would not do to run in that direction. Only one hope remained, and it was seemingly diminishing as the dark outlines of the forests of Isla de Pinos were growing clearer. The Lincoln must get behind the coral reefs or she must fall a victim to her pursuer.

"Aunt Valencia," said Esmeralda, "they have ceased firing."

"O, my darling!" exclaimed the matron, folding the beautiful girl to her bosom. "I fear it is only because they now feel sure of overtaking us! Worse than death!"

"We shall not be captured," hoarsely whispered Esmeralda. "I shall not!"

"Neither shall I!" said the señora.

Both of them put their hands to their sides, for they each had on a belt from which hung a heavy revolver in its leather case. The men had laughed approvingly on seeing the belts, and they had said to each other:

"Two more fighters! Plucky women!"

But the women's thoughts went further. Only too many tales had been told in their hearing concerning the dealings of the chivalry of Spain with Cuban rebel captives.

"They think they will have us pretty soon," said Captain Griswold, on the after deck. "Less than two miles now, but the point of that reef is a matter they must steer away from. That shot fell pretty near."

He did not know that it was the last cartridge of the gunboat's best gun, or that he was now nearly within fair reaching distance of her smaller pieces.

Within fifteen minutes these also were beginning to try their luck, and more than one critic upon the deck of the Lincoln was induced to remark, in English or Spanish or some other tongue:

"What wretched gunnery!"

"It won't be long now," said Stevens to himself, but he was standing near one of the torpedo tubes between decks, and Captain Griswold was coming down the companionway.

"The Commodore told me this was said to have a possibly longer range," he heard Jack say. "Glad they are not all alike. As we tack at the reef, we shall turn this broadside to him. I'll try it!"

"Look out, captain!" said Stevens. "You know what you are doing."

"No, I don't," said Jack. "I can't tell yet. But they've shown us their good will, and it's time for us to be polite. That beggar westerly has come up rapidly. It's a large cruiser. Draws more water than we do or a gunboat."

"Glad you're so cool about it," said the mate, with a darkening face. "Every life on board'll answer for this."

"Never you mind!" said Jack. "We were all forfeited long ago, if they take us. You and all the rest of us."

There was a sound of danger to somebody in the tone of that remark, but the copper torpedo case was going in at the breech of the gun. Then its piratical, filibustering gunner stooped and squinted, muttering orders to his aids, and waiting for the right motion of the ship.

"Struck!" shouted voices on deck. "Hit us twice! Neither of them went through."

"Light shot," said Jack. "Now! Fire!"

A louder report than had been made by the tube on deck and a greater jar of the frame of the Lincoln.

"Aunt Valencia!" exclaimed Esmeralda. "Jack is firing at them."

"You mean Captain Griswold, my dear," said her aunt reprovingly. "Please be more careful."

"Madame!" shouted Mike Donnelly. "Look yonder! He hit their smoke pipe! Busted! No great harrum to them, I'm afraid, but it'll tache 'em a lesson. Hurrah, b'yes!"

A loud cheer went up from the men, but upon the Spanish gunboat there was sudden consternation. Not that any important injury had been done to their vessel, but that half a dozen of their crew lay dead or wounded by the flying fragments of the Yankee shell.

"Caramba! She's armed!" roared the captain. "We must wait for the cruiser. Fire away! Give it to her."

His light guns were indeed worked with considerable energy, but the Lincoln was not likely to pay any especial attention to them, for the gunboat was manifestly lessening her speed.

"I won't try again, right away," said Griswold. "I'm wanted on deck just now."

Up he went, and there did not seem to be anything for him to do, but Mate Stevens lifted a pointing hand and said:

"Look yonder, captain. What do you think of that?"

Puffs of smoke were showing upon the far-away Spanish man-of-war. The roar of heavy guns quickly followed, but whatever missiles went with it found only the sea for a target.

"All right," said Jack. "They have plenty

of ammunition. I'm not afraid of that fellow. We can lose him among the keys.''

''Perhaps we can,'' said Mate Stevens. ''But our chances are pretty thin.''

''Stop your croaking,'' snarled Mike Donnelly. ''Ye're an owl! Sure, the captain's bate off the gunboat. What do we care for wan cloomsy cruiser?''

''She carries long range guns,'' said Stevens.

CHAPTER XI

"We are running our best, señorita."

"O, Captain Griswold, don't let them overtake us! The great ship is nearer."

"Because we must take this course for a little distance further," said Jack. "We shall turn easterly in a few minutes. I have no doubt——"

"O, my God!"

"Captain!"

"O, Jack! They are killed! Torn in pieces!"

Most of the men on deck had drifted aft to watch their pursuers, but there had been a small group near the prow. Of these not a man was left alive, for a shell from the cruiser had exploded among them. It had been from a small bore, rapid-fire gun, and its flying fragments had done no harm to the Lincoln, but here were six mangled corpses of Cuban refugees.

245

"Down to the cabin and the hold!" All who are not on duty!" shouted Jack. "I'll try them with the long tube."

The deck was quickly cleared, but Esmeralda fainted at the companionway, and Jack had to carry her down to the cabin.

"O, what horror!" she exclaimed, as her dark eyes opened, staringly. "I never before saw bloodshed. It is dreadful!"

"A solid shot glanced from the side, aft, just now," reported Mike from above. "They have our range. It's tight papers. I'm afraid we're a goner."

"Tell Cannara to go ahead!" shouted Jack. "Put on all steam! We won't surrender."

Señora Valencia was now in charge of Esmeralda, and Jack stepped to his gun. A torpedo was already in it, and in a moment more he was sighting—sighting, trying to make sure of that shot.

On deck all was quiet, for the dead were overboard and the living were lying flat upon the deck, all but one.

"This is of no use, Cannara," said Mate Stevens to the steersman. "Head her for the cruiser. I've ordered the engineer to slow up. Around with her!"

He thought he had given such an order through the second mate, one Michael Donnelly, but it must have been misunderstood, for the Lincoln was even increasing her already high speed. The Carib must have heard, but he only showed his white, grinding teeth, and took one hand from the wheel for an instant to loosen the long knife in his belt.

"Didn't you hear me?" shouted Stevens.

"I did. Let him alone. I've the captain's orders to shoot any man that meddles with the steering."

"I'm in command on deck."

"I'm Colonel Valencia. Men! Your rifles!"

"This is mutiny!" roared Stevens.

Bang! At that moment the ship quivered with the concussion of the long torpedo tube, and there was a moment of waiting.

"Splendid marksman!" exclaimed the Colonel; "but he cannot harm that big fellow."

Perhaps not, for she was partly armored, and the torpedo was not large, but its gun elevation had been considerable, to get the range and it went up in a sweeping curve to alight upon the deck of the Spaniard.

Blood for blood this time. Twice more than man for man. A huge hole in the deck itself, where it went through to spread its bursting ruin among a crowd of all sorts between decks. There had been no armor in its way. Only wood, and the splinters of this had also done much damage.

A broadside hastily responded, but angry firing is not always good shooting, and the Lincoln went on as if she had a charmed life.

"Ye born divil!" shouted Mike to Stevens. "They'd shoot ivery wan of us! I'll go down fightin'. Wan worrud more about surrender, and ye're a dead man. Here comes the captain."

"Stevens, are you mad?" asked Jack, very quietly. "What do you mean?"

"I mean, are you mad, and all of the men?" responded Stevens. "If you had any sense left you would see that I am right. This is destruction!"

"You will give no more orders on this ship," said Jack. "Go below! I'll save your cowardly life if I can, but you're no man for a sea-fight. Go! Men, let him alone. I'll care for the ship."

Stevens' face was livid as he turned away, but he retained his firmness wonderfully.

"I am right!" he said. "You are only throwing away the ship and every life on board of her. I'm acquitted of all the consequences."

"You are," said Jack. "I'll take all the responsibility."

Down went Stevens, followed by black looks and curses, but there were not wanting those among the crew who said to one another:

"There's a good deal of reason in his way of looking at it. We can't escape."

Roar on roar came from the cruiser, and heavy shell came very near, but the distance between the two vessels was now again increasing.

Great had been the astonishment on the Spanish cruiser, but there was little fear of a second success like that, for the Spanish gunners and her officers did but make the air blue with curses and hot threats of vengeance. They were now again signalling their own gunboat, and she was inceasing her speed in spite of the rent in her smoke pipe and the possible coming of something worse.

"Colonel," said Captain Griswold, "we have made a long run since daylight, but we were further in then than I supposed. Look ahead!"

"Islands!" exclaimed the Colonel. "Safety!"

"Not quite yet," said Jack; "but if that cruiser draws twenty feet, and we only ten, she had better not follow us into a shallow channel."

"Shoaling!" came at that moment from a man at the sounding line. "By the mark, four!"

"Going over a sunken ledge," responded Cannara. "Deep, over there. Then I show you. She dare not come."

Shots were every now and then spraying the waves around the Lincoln, but the captain of the cruiser probably knew something of that navigation. He was not willing to risk the loss of his ship, and he was slowing as well as firing. The range was getting longer, and his gunnery seemed to be getting worse. At all events, Jack had no more immediate use for his torpedo tubes, except that a solitary shot went back at the gunboat from his "stern chaser." She was not hit this time, but the torpedo did not fall short, and the warning may have been worth something. Nearer and nearer were a number of low-lying coral reef islands, over some of whose beaches high breakers were foaming. It was a dangerous looking coast to steer for, but Cannara's white teeth showed in expectant laughter as he steered steadily on.

"Captain," he replied to a somewhat anxious question, "all coast men know channel here. Gunboat pilot know. He follow right through. Cruiser no follow. Captain whip gunboat."

"I don't know about that," said Jack. "We will get into the lagoon, and run for the second line of islands."

"So!" said Cannara. "Bad place in dark. No light. Strike reef. Too many rock."

"You are right about that," said Jack, "but we have almost thrown off the cruiser."

"No!" exclaimed Cannara. "Big Spaniard go to other channel. Go through. Try to catch us in lagoon."

"Our only chance, then," said Jack, "is to make three knots to her two while we can."

Word went down that the deck was safe again, and the two women came up, but they shuddered as they looked forward to the now well washed spot where the six men had fallen. Then they glanced back at the pursuing gunboat and the far-away cruiser.

"Captain Griswold," said Esmeralda, "are we getting away from them?"

"For this time, yes," he replied. "We are to run between these two islands, but nobody knows what we may find beyond them."

"O, dear!" exclaimed Señora Valencia. "We may see more Spanish men-of-war."

"I think not, señora," said Jack. "There are not so many of them. They can't be everywhere."

"Revenue cutters and guarda costas," suggested the Colonel.

"We can blow them out of the water, my dear friend," said Jack. "That's what we will do, too."

CHAPTER XII

"A narrow passage, but we may get through. Reefs, reefs, reefs, as dangerous as the guns of the Spaniards. That shot went over us."

Mate Stevens was again on deck, and he was watching the changed condition of things as calmly as ever.

"What if we had surrendered?" asked Jack. "We'd all have been shot by this time. We shall soon be safe."

"I don't think they would have shot anybody but Cubans but for our firing," said Stevens. "I will answer to the Commodore and to the government for my opinion. The law is on my side."

"I'm no sea lawyer," said Jack. "The captain of that cruiser won't trouble himself about any law."

"Not now, he won't," replied Stevens. "I'm with you. Our only chance for our lives is to go ahead. I'll fight. But I stick to it that I was right at first.''

"Who cares?'' said Jack. ''The ledges themselves are as good as earthworks, or better, against those heavy shell. We are safer every minute.''

"Captain!'' exclaimed Stevens. ''I'm a sailor. The cruiser is heading for the northerly passage. Don't deceive yourself. And the gunboat is following us.''

"And the night is drawing nearer,'' put in Colonel Valencia. ''Nobody disputes you when you say we are not yet out of danger.''

Exceedingly plausible had been the arguments of the first mate, but they would have been more so if the Lincoln had not been a marked and doomed vessel from the hour she left New York. She had no business to be in those waters ''on her way to Vera Cruz, Mexico,'' with a cargo of contraband of war and a lot of Cuban refugees for passengers. To all Spanish eyes and before military judges she was little better, if any, than a pirate, for whom there could be no mercy.

Before long that lot of little islands was behind her, and another could be dimly discerned in the distance. Here, however, was a wide reach of open sea, and steam could safely be put on again. The big cruiser was not only out of range, but out of sight, and the gunboat was picking her way among the reefs with circumspection.

"Now's our time!" shouted Jack to Cannara at the wheel. "Due north!"

"Right into the jaws of the cruiser!" exclaimed Stevens. "What for?"

"To let that higher island hide our smoke, if you must know," said Jack. "We're going to make something out of the night when it comes. I believe we can whip that gunboat at short range. I'll take care of the cruiser."

"All is lost by his rashness," muttered Stevens, as he turned away, and he was again aware that some of the crew silently agreed with him. They could hardly believe that a mere yachtsman could be a better captain than an old salt who had commanded traders heretofore in these very seas. Besides, their necks were at risk, and the chances seemed to be against them. Nevertheless, they were greatly in the minority, and they went on about their duties gloomily.

An hour went by, and now the smoke of the pursuing gunboat could no longer be seen.

"So far, so good!" remarked Jack to Esmeralda, standing beside him on the deck. "Señorita, we have now only about forty miles to run."

"Is there any hope?" she exclaimed. "I had almost begun to despair."

"No time for that yet," he cheerily responded. "You will be on shore in Cuba by daylight to-morrow morning."

That was said aloud, but his thoughts added: "Or else at the bottom of the sea."

He left her and went to the wheelhouse for a chat with Cannara, and Señora Valencia said to her:

"I thought you were so courageous?"

"So I am," said Esmeralda, "but I have such a strange feeling all over me. It isn't fear exactly, but I seem to feel that there is something awful about to happen."

"I don't believe in presentiments," replied her aunt. "Thus far, we have escaped wonderfully. But isn't Captain Griswold a brave fellow!"

"He is splendid!" exclaimed Esmeralda. "He seems to be made of iron."

He was not so exactly, for as he stood and

glanced back at her a great shudder went over him, and he hoarsely muttered:

"Better she were at the bottom of the sea. Far better dead than captured by such beasts as these Spanish officers."

To all appearance, the bold trick of seeming to run toward the track of the cruiser had temporarily succeeded. She would have miles to lose in finding her deep water passage, and even there her progress could not be at her best speed. O for darkness!

That was what almost everybody on board the Lincoln was thinking, or even saying when the man at the forward lookout shouted:

"Boat! Captain! Large one. Got a gun. Headed for us."

A mile away as yet was the stranger. Glasses quickly aimed at her made her out as large as the long boat of a man-of-war. She was full of armed men, and she carried a Spanish flag.

"Guarda costa," said the Colonel. "One of the patrol boats. There are many of them."

"Her cannon is a six-pounder popgun," said Captain Griswold. "I don't want to fire and let the cruiser know where we are. It's getting darker. No rowboat can catch us, but she's in our way. Cannara, easterly two points.''

Hardly had the propeller changed her course in so plain an attempt to escape before the boat gun spoke out, and a round shot came skipping along over the water.

"No harrum, yer honor," sang out Mike; "but the noise of her."

"That's the devil of it!" growled Jack, for hardly had the report of the boat gun died away before a heavier detonation muffled by distance answered it from the southern horizon.

"The cruiser!" whispered Esmeralda to her aunt. "Now they know where we are."

"Shall you reply?" asked Stevens.

"No!" said Jack. "I don't want to murder those fools in the boat. I'll let 'em get away. We're doing well enough."

The boat was a swift one, well pulled, however, and even the course of the Lincoln was bringing it nearer.

"Captain," said the Colonel, shortly afterward, "they have wasted four cannon balls. They are within long rifle range. Let the men pepper them."

"Go it!" said Jack. "They won't hit anybody. Let them have some sea rifle practice."

A hundred, at least, of the latest pattern of
long range rifles were very quickly on deck,
and as many eager men were peering along
the black barrels. Then followed a sharp, con-
tinuous cracking for a minute or so, while the
telescopes and binoculars watched for results.

"I declare!" exclaimed Jack. "I didn't
expect it, but such a shower of bullets——"

"Hit!" shouted the Colonel. "They
couldn't all miss. Keep it up, men."

There was indeed a sudden commotion
among the somewhat closely packed crew of
the Spanish guarda costa, or patrol boat, or
whatever she was. Two men dropped their
oars, and another sprang suddenly overboard.

Shouts and yells and curses rang out, and
there was a pause in the rowing. One more
useless shot was fired from the boat gun, but
the rattle of rifles had not ceased and the bullets were dropping dangerously near all the
while. It was very fair long range shooting,
but not exactly Creedmoor work.

Another man went down, one of the gunners, and the officer in command of the boat
shouted to his oarsmen to pull as rapidly as

possible out of that leaden rain. He had had enough.

He had also done enough to have ruined the Lincoln if he had done it earlier in the day. Now, however, as the signal guns of the cruiser and the gunboat replied again to each other, the Yankee pirate once more resumed her northerly course, a full hour, hidden by deepening shadows. Then her speed gradually lessened, and she seemed to be feeling her way.

Captain Griswold was forward, watching the sailor who was casting the sounding lead, when a hand gently touched his arm and he was asked:

"Jack, are we safe?"

He turned and looked sadly into her eyes for a moment before he responded:

"No, Esmeralda. Pray to God, if you know how. I can't say that I do. We are among the keys on the south line of the Golfo de Matamano. The cruiser is less than a mile behind us. We dare not go faster."

"Jack!" she exclaimed, "neither dare they."

The light of his lantern was falling clearly upon her beautiful face, and he saw in it a terrible expression of desperation as she added:

"Go on! Better the sharks among the reefs than the Spaniards."

There was a slight sound of grating along the keel at that moment.

"Struck!" shouted Stevens. "All is lost!"

"Over! Hurrah!" loudly answered the voice of the leadsman. "Deep water, Captain."

"Safe, Esmeralda," whispered Jack. "We have won five miles upon them, but the tide was falling. We had not an inch to spare. A little later we should have grounded or had a hole knocked in the bottom—All right!"

His last shout was to the anxious crew and passengers, and even the cheers they tried to reply with were somewhat faint. Then it was as if the cruiser fired a shell at that cheering, but the boom of her gun had no harm in it.

"Steady, Cannara——"

"Ten miles deep water," said the Carib.

"Then westward to the point. The cruiser cannot run in there. They will lose us now in the dark."

At all events, the big Spaniard was coming no further in a straight line, for her commander knew all about that dangerous line of coral ledges. It was a good place to keep away from.

CHAPTER XIII

THE FIGHT AT THE LANDING

Anxious nights pass slowly, but their long hours will wear away. The dawn of the next day brightened in a sky without a cloud, and it came to an utter silence upon a place on the southern coast of Cuba. It was more like a land-locked lagoon than a cove, for a rocky spur of a high promontory shut it in. Away to the easterly was an opening to tell how a ship might have entered, but a steersman unacquainted with the coast might easily have sailed past it without discovering it, especially in the night or in thick weather.

"As good as a North River pier, Captain," shouted Mike Donnelly, staring at the rocky edges of the shore westerly. "We've sounded all along. She can lie close up to the ledge. Three fathom to the straight face of it. The derricks can swing things right ashore."

Captain Griswold was eagerly scanning the wooded shore line, and he did not at once reply. Every soul on board was on deck, except the engineers and stokers, and every man had his rifle ready. Further along the surface of the promontory was bare of large trees, as if it had once been cultivated, and upon its ridge were the fire-blackened ruins of a building.

"Santa Maria!" murmured Esmeralda. "Here is our last danger."

"I hope it is," said Jack. "Donnelly, up with the anchors, and bring her to her shore berth. We must unload as fast as we can. Colonel!"

"I shall go into the woods with my men and scout forward," said the Colonel. "Our friends ought not to be far away. But it would be of little use to land the torpedo tubes here."

"That is what we must do," said Jack, "if we come back from Vera Cruz after them. We mustn't have them on board when we get there. They'd convict us."

"They could lie here safely enough," said the Colonel. "But you had better leave them somewhere else."

"I'll see," said Jack, and shortly the propeller was slowly working her way to the side of the natural wharf, so like a thousand others in that peculiar formation.

The moment she was moored the Colonel and his men sprang out eagerly, rifle in hand, and the crew of the Lincoln were already busy with the cargo. The muzzle of one torpedo tube eyed the shore from the cabin window, and the two others on deck, fore and aft, turned their heads landward, as if ready to throw something at a Spaniard.

"Señor Griswold, I am going ashore!"

"No, Señorita Gonzales! Not yet. Wait until we are sure all is safe."

"I will go with her. Only a little distance," said the Colonel's wife. "We are wild to put our feet upon our own island. We will hurry back if there is any warning of danger."

"I cannot object to that," he said. "Do not go far. We suppose that our own friends occupy this neighborhood."

"I must!" urged Esmeralda, and in a moment more the two women were walking along leisurely under the trees that seemed so peacefully shady.

The mainland arose with a long, gentle slope from the water's edge. Here, too, were signs of former occupation, but instead of cultivated fields there were now brambles and weeds and luxuriant bushes. In among these had Colonel Valencia led his men, advancing cautiously, and at first no signs of human life presented themselves.

"Halt!" commanded the Colonel. "Away yonder on the ridge is the old rifle-pit where we beat them two years ago. It seems to be unoccupied now. We will explore that, and if all is safe we may tell Griswold our landing is unsuspected."

Three of the men went forward under cover toward the ridge. From many things which had been said, on shipboard and now, it appeared that more than one cargo had been landed in this neighborhood. Perhaps it was less likely to be watched with so active a naval force in the offing, but there could not be too much caution exercised.

"Hark!" suddenly exclaimed Valencia. "Look! The scouts are running! Drop under cover. Every man to his tree if he can find one."

The three scouts had actually entered what may once have been a respectable earthwork, but which bore no signs of ever having been defended by cannon. It was large enough for a regiment. They looked hastily around and hurried across to the further front. The work was breast high, with a ditch beyond.

"Horsemen! Our own cavalry!" exclaimed one of the men.

"Running! They are pursued!"

"We must warn the Colonel! Back!"

Not at all in good order, but every man for himself, about two hundred mounted men dashed out from under the cover of a line of trees half a mile away. No sooner were they well out, however, before they wheeled and sent back a scattering volley at a throng of brilliant Spanish uniforms which began to show in the edge of the same woods. It was returned, and two or three Cubans fell from their horses, while the rest rode on.

Out poured the pursuers, evidently a strong body of regular cavalry, and they halted a moment to form in good order before advancing.

"Our fellows mean to make a stand here," said one of the scouts. "The Colonel might reinforce them. On! Quick!"

The rattle of shots had warned Colonel Valencia, but by the time the scouts reached him it was too late to lead his men to the redoubt. The mounted Cubans indeed rode in, dismounted and took position behind the breastwork. They were not instantly attacked. The Spanish commander wisely refrained from a cavalry dash at such a stronghold. Besides he seemed to have another errand, for he did not even halt. He wheeled his column, possibly of about four hundred, away to the right of the earthwork, and they went on at a brisk trot.

"The landing!" groaned Valencia, "that is their aim! Madre di Dios! They will capture the Lincoln! Give them a volley!"

Sharp and close was the shooting at barely three hundred yards, but it was a flanking fire and it did but send the cavalry faster, although a number of saddles were emptied. An unknown, ambushed enemy may have seemed to the Spanish officer worse to ride in upon than a redoubt.

At the landing the firing had been heard.

"Mike!" shouted Jack. "I'll go after her! Man the guns! Men! Rifles! Be ready."

"Aunt!" exclaimed Esmeralda. "Hark! To the ship, darling! Run! The Spaniards are coming! O God!"

They turned, breathlessly to retrace their

imprudent steps, but Stevens had sprung ashore when Griswold did, as if he, too, meant to be heroic. But the half-uttered words on his lips were:

"Now's my chance! If I don't escape now I never shall. I hope they've sent force enough this time."

He ran well, but Jack was ahead of him, and he was the first to meet the affrighted women.

"Jack!"

"Esmeralda! Señora Valencia! O my Esmeralda!"

"Jack! They are coming!"

"Surrender, Captain!" shouted Stevens. "There they are. They won't hurt the ladies."

In full view was the head of the now closely serried Spanish column, and a wild cheer went up as the foremost riders caught sight of the Lincoln.

"We have her!" shouted the commander.

"The prize is won! Forward!"

There were sailors, however, who had rifles, and they were using them well at so short a range.

"Surrender Griswold, you fool!" roared Stevens, in a commanding tone. "It's all over with you and your boat. These are my friends. Give me that girl."

"Jack! Darling!"

There was a sharp report as Griswold's rifle came to his shoulder, and the treacherous mate staggered and fell.

"Now for a Spaniard," hissed Jack, as he turned and fired again, but there were louder sounds than rifle shots.

"Here goes!" groaned Mike, at the cabin gun. "But what's to bust the shell? It's no good!"

Little he knew of torpedoes. The horse of a cavalryman was quite enough to explode the sensitive cap at the point of that terrible, long shell, and the guncotton did its work. Another shell from the after gun struck a tree and exploded. Only the shot from the forward tube went through the column harmlessly.

"O, Captain, she has fallen!"

"I've a shot in my arm! God help us!"

The crew were plying their rifles, but the cavalry had had enough. The work of the torpedoes had been deadly among so dense a throng. Horses and men went down in rows.

"The Major's dead!" they shouted. "Artillery! It's a massacre! Ride! Run!"

Go they did, pell-mell, only to pass again within pistol shot of Colonel Valencia's ambush, and receive a couple of rattling volleys doing fatal execution.

"It's beaten they are," growled Mike. "But I wanted to give thim another pill. O, the Captain! I'm afraid they got to him! The b'ye! And his pretty colleen, too!"

He sprang up to the deck, but a dozen brawny sailors had gone ashore already without waiting for orders.

"Señora, can you lift her on that side? I can use one arm."

"She's not hurt, I hope! Esmeralda!"

The dark, beautiful eyes opened.

"O, aunt! Jack! Was he killed? I saw him drop his rifle! Is he dead?"

"Indeed I'm not," whispered Jack, his right arm all as strong as ever tightening around her. "A shot hit you?"

"No, it hit you," she said. "I fainted. Are they gone? The Spaniards?"

"Why, my darling, we've beaten them."

"O! I can stand," she said. "I am all right, Captain Griswold."

"Boys," said Jack to his arriving sailors, "tie up my left arm. Cut the sleeve. The bone's not broken. Tie tightly above the wound. It's not an artery. Tighter! There!'' and he in turn grew deadly white and fell, but Mike Donnelly kindly explained to Esmeralda:

"It's not so much the bullet in his arrum, miss, as it was his fright about yirsilf. It's enough to knock over ony man to have his girl in such danger.''

The flight of the Spanish cavalry was a rout, for their losses had been very severe. They had not even discovered the strength of their foes, and were therefore free to report them at several thousands, whom they had "dispersed with much slaughter, only two men being killed and three wounded among the heroes of Spain.''

CHAPTER XIV

Colonel Valencia and his riflemen were now in the earthwork, exchanging enthusiastic greetings with their fellow-patriots.

"It will not do to remain here," they were told; "but horses can be brought in any number. We can carry our supplies and so forth to places of safety. But the ladies! This torn-up province is no place for them. You were crazy, Colonel, to bring your wife here."

"She would come with me!" he said. "So would Miss Gonzales. I could not help it."

"Nonsense!" his friends replied. "We will send for young Captain Gonzales. He and her mother can be here by the day after to-morrow. His brother is away in Puerto Principe. Cuba just now is a place for fighting men, not for any more women."

As for the Spanish cavalry, they were not at all likely to return without strong reinforcements, and the patriots would therefore have a day or so for unmolested work.

"Now," said the Colonel, "I must go to the ship. Come along, a hundred of you. Let us know at once if there are any signs of trouble here. But how they did scatter at the first roar of Griswold's artillery!"

Not until he arrived at the water side did he learn how terrible had been the work of the torpedoes or how narrow had been the risk of utter ruin.

"The Captain?" he exclaimed. "Wounded?"

"Not so bad as we thought at first, sir," replied Mike Donnelly. "It's his left arrum is tore, but it's doing well. He won't be put anywhere but on deck, and we've put an awning for him. The leddies is with him."

Forward strode the Colonel, and he was quickly enough on board. A stirring scene was before him, for every pair of hands that could be utilized was busy with getting out the hidden cargo and preparing to land it in all haste.

"Captain!" shouted Valencia. "O! This is too bad! How is your arm?"

"Neither bone nor artery touched," replied Jack, cheerfully. "I am a little weak from loss of blood. Less fever to follow for that reason, I suppose. The ball was not a ragged one, and went right through. I must be careful. Tell me about the fight.''

''Don't talk too much, John.''

''O! It's John, is it?'' he laughed.

''Husband!'' exclaimed Señora Valencia; ''I must tell you first—'' And tell him she did, while his face whitened at the story of her narrow escape.

''That settles it!'' he shouted. ''You and Esmeralda are going right back in the propeller. This is no place for you. Even the eastern provinces are only half safe. Esmeralda, it would be wicked for you to leave him! Think of the anxiety! I know what that would be.''

Griswold turned a little faintly and his usually cold face flushed as if with a great spasm of fever pain.

''John! Does it hurt you?''

''Yes, Esmeralda. I mean, Señorita Gonzales.''

''Esmeralda, John.''

''It pains me dreadfully! I could not bare to leave you here. I could not live! I should die.''

''I will go with you!'' she whispered. ''Don't say any more just now.''

274

"But we have sent for her brother and her mother," interrupted the Colonel, and then followed the whole account of the fight beyond the ridge.

"It is so strange," murmured Esmeralda, "to come all the way to Cuba and fight one battle and go right back to New York again."

"One?" said her uncle. "Think of our naval exploits. We have beaten them at sea as well as upon the land."

"That's a thing we may have to do again," said Jack. "We will keep our torpedo tubes on deck until we are in the Gulf of Mexico. But we will deliver the rest of our cargo at New Orleans instead of Vera Cruz. The Commodore can arrange all that for us by telegraph after we get there."

"After you get there!" exclaimed the Colonel, doubtfully. "For the first few days I shall be safer on the land than you will be on the sea. Now, you lie still and Donnelly and I will attend to all this affair."

"What are those fellows doing in yonder?" inquired Jack.

"O!" said Valencia, "I'm an old campaigner. Any kind of fence, of logs, branches, stones, earth, is a good help against cavalry."

"Good to hinder infantry, too," said Jack. "They are making it pretty strong.

"Before to-morrow morning," said the Colonel, "that frail breastwork will be equal to doubling our force. Only a very strong attacking party would care to walk up to it. You could send shells right over the men in it."

"We have a few ordinary shells that will fit," said Jack. "They are coming on deck. We can use them, if need be, at so short a range as that. Better than torpedoes for this business."

So the talk ceased, for after the Colonel turned away to his duties Jack was compelled to lie still. Curiously not a soul seemed disposed to say anything about Mate Stevens. It was carefully left to be supposed that he had been killed by a shot from the Spanish cavalry, except that Mike replied to one of the men:

"Shut up, ye divil! What do you know about war? The Captain had a repeatin' rifle an' he was blazin' at every inemy he could see. Good shot, too!"

"All I know is, Mike," said the sailor, "he saved me the throuble. I've had me eye on that traitor all along. He'd sold us out, and he was on his way to jine his buyers. That's all, me bye.''

"He didn't get to 'em," said Mike.

All day long and into the night the unloading and carrying away went rapidly on. Trains of pack-horses and mules came and went, but there was no use for wheels.

The awning on deck was cooler than the cabin, and Jack lay where he could see what was going on, but he was not allowed to interfere. Neither was he at any moment left alone.

It was under a bright moonlight that was shining, an hour or so before the coming of another day, that a mounted party came dashing to the landing, hardly answering the loud hails which greeted them at the now quite respectable breastwork. Nevertheless, anybody could hear:

"I am Gonzales! My mother! Where is my sister?"

"On board, sir! Ride in! He was wounded bad in the fight. She's tendin' her man, sir, and a good man he is."

"Her man? I must see to this."

"Juan, my son, wait!"

"Mother, Esmeralda is my sister. The Colonel sent no word of this."

"Hurrah!" shouted the voice of Valencia, at that moment. "Captain, they are here. Esmeralda, wake up! Your mother!"

"Mother! Come! Juan, is it you? O, mother, Jack was shot through the arm in the fight. I was so foolish to go out as I did. He might have been killed!"

The arrivals dismounted quickly, and they were met at the gang-plank by the Colonel with a tremendous welcome.

"Juan Gonzales," he said, "here comes Esmeralda. Don't be alarmed. Your brother-in-law will soon get well. You'll be proud of him."

"O!" said Juan, suddenly mollified. "I must see him at once."

His next experience, however, was a wild hug from his sister, and a rapid story of her adventures, winding up with:

"O, Juan, Jack says that mother must come with us. He means to get us to New York, and then he is to join the American army that's to fight for Cuba."

"What?" exclaimed Juan. "An army from the United States to join us?"

"Not a doubt of it," said Valencia. "Is it possible that you do not know?"

"We hear almost nothing."

It was a fact! Not until that moment had this part of the Cuban patriot forces heard anything of the destruction of the Maine or of the war feeling in the United States.

"Hurrah!" shouted Juan. "We shall be free! Our deliverance has come! We may now fight on with some hope."

But he strode forward eagerly to the awning and exclaimed:

"Griswold! My brave friend!"

"I heard you," said Jack. "I am so glad Señora Gonzales came. She must return with me. Talk with Esmeralda; I am faint just now. I must rest. I must be able to command when we sail."

"I am afraid you will not," returned young Gonzales. "It will be a perilous trip. I'll see her and I'll talk with you again."

"Not now," interposed the Colonel. "All this has been too much for him. He needs a sleep. Ugh! How hot it is!"

There were mosquitoes, too, as well as perils by land and sea, but the military cargo had

now been landed, all but the tell-tale armament of the Lincoln.

The day dawned, but when it came all the
women were in their state-rooms, and Juan
Gonzales sat by the heavily slumbering Captain.

"Your honor," said Mike Donnelly, in a
whisper, "aisy with him. We're gettin' up
stame."

"You are to sail at once?" asked the Cuban
patriot.

"It's our only chance, he said before he
wint to slape. The Spanish cruisers 'll head
us off."

"Go, then, by all means!" exclaimed Juan.

"Of course, they must," added Colonel
Valencia, from behind him. "I've been down
saying good-bye. You and I and our friends
must be far away before sunset. A Spanish
column is reported."

Silent was the slumbering Captain, and with
as little noise as might be his crew completed
their preparations. There were weeping fare-
wells below, and then Colonel Gonzales and
his nephew came on deck.

"I'll wake him," said Mike. "Captain
Jack! They're goin'! Spake to'em."

His eyes opened, but few enough were the words that passed, even then.

"Colonel," said Jack, at last, "by the time the Lincoln reaches New York, war will be declared. I shall leave your wife and my wife behind me; for, on the water or on the land, I mean to be among the first United States forces that strike for the freedom of Cuba."

"God bless you!" they said. "Come!"

Then he was alone for awhile, and they and all that remained of the Cuban horsemen and footmen were hurrying far away with the precious supplies from the Lincoln.

CHAPTER XV

"It's the stowage, Captain; we are com-
plating that," said Mate Donnelly, a few hours
later.

"Cast off the moorings at all events," said
the Captain. "Run her out sixty yards from
the shore. There's no time to lose. We may
be attacked at any moment."

"Aye, aye, sir," said Mike, and the Lincoln
was speedily free of the shore, but she was
hardly ready for a voyage.

"No passengers this time," the sailors said,
"but we're enough men for a fight.'

"Betther for a run," said Mike.

The motion of the vessel may have oper-
ated as a summons, for now the somewhat
tearful women came hurrying on deck.

"Oh, Cuba! Cuba!" exclaimed Señora
Gonzales, mournfully. "I did not wish to
leave it. Farewell, Cuba!"

"Captain!" said Señora Valencia, "are we
really off?"

"Nearly, thank God!" he began, but he instantly shouted: "Esmeralda! All of you! Go below! Look yonder! Robinson, swing around that forward gun. No anchoring! Cannara, steer for the inlet! Donnelly—fire! Men, rifles! Give it to them!"

Fiercely rapid were his orders, for the shell instantly sent from the after gun by Donnelly burst among a swarm of Spanish foot-soldiers surging against the brushwood and rubbish of the breastwork. Already they were opening a musketry fire, and it would be at short range. The shell checked them for a moment, and another followed it.

Down again hurried the women, and a third roar was heard from the starboard cabin window.

"Those shells were well placed," said Jack, coolly. "Three of my men down? Scores of Spaniards. Here we go. She's gaining headway. All hands below! Under cover, every man!"

"Ye'll go doon yoursilf, thin," shouted Mike, and strong hands carried the wounded commander below, whether he would or not.

All the while the leaden hail rattled against

283

the steel sides of the propeller, but Cannara in the wheelhouse seemed to bear a charmed life. Bullets struck all around him, but none of them hit him. The torpedo tubes on deck were deserted, for their gunners would easily have been picked off by the marksmen on shore. The larboard cabin tube sent another shell among these, with deadly effect, but the main object was to get away, and there was no lingering for useless fighting.

"Neither do I want too much cannonading," said Jack to Esmeralda. "But, O! how I wish we could have waited for night! We have yet an hour of daylight and of danger."

"We are together," she said. "I have been praying. It seems to me that my evil presentiments are all gone."

"Why, my dear," said Jack, "that was your natural scare about the Spanish cruisers and our landing. You have actually been to Cuba now, and you have brought away your mother. You have seen your brother, too."

"Thanks to you," she said. "But now I want to get mother in safety to New York. I'm really more afraid than ever."

"I think those fellows on shore can do us no more harm," replied Jack. "So glad they didn't kill Cannara! What could we do without him!''

The Spanish infantry, mad with disappointment, were still blazing away, when the stars and stripes on the flagstaff of the Lincoln disappeared around the point of rocks at the entrance of the lagoon.

"A clear sea!" shouted down the mate, after a hasty glance from the deck. "Not a sail or a smoke in sight."

"Leave the heading of her to Cannara," replied Griswold. "Put on steam! Ho, for the Gulf and for New Orleans!"

An hour passed by, and the longed-for darkness came. The Lincoln showed no lights, and every wandering spark which at times went up from her pipes was something to be dreaded. It seemed as if nobody cared to stay below, and the very men spoke to each other in hushed voices.

"Every mile counts," Mike was saying, when a sailor touched his elbow.

"It's a light on the lee bow," he whispered. "Tell the Captain."

Jack was already watching the far-away glimmer when the report was made.

"Can you make it out at all?" asked Mike.

"I can," said Jack. "The fools have told us pretty plainly. That is, if they have any idea we are coming."

"What is it, then?" exclaimed Esmeralda.

"Two lanterns, fore and aft," he said. "And the distance between them tells of a long keel. The only vessel of that size in these waters would be a Spanish gunboat. We are headed for her now."

"Shall we change our course?" asked Mike. "It's about time, then."

"Not a point," replied his Captain. "Cannara is steering for the nearest islands. He knows a passage. Our hope is in silence and no lanterns. Cover every light on board."

That had already been done, and the very propeller herself seemed disposed to move with the least possible noise. All steam was on, however, and she was plowing swiftly through a quiet sea.

"A bloody trip!" Jack muttered. "Four of our crew killed. Six of the Cubans. On this very deck. Ghastly work among the Spaniards on shore. Stevens dead; I'm wounded. And now here comes—we are discovered! Hark!"

The boom of a heavy gun!

"Are they crazy, to think that we would heave to?" he shouted. "Steady, Cannara! Don't vary from your course."

"We're within a mile of 'em," said Mike. "They're coming."

"Get the guns ready!" commanded Jack. "Bear on their lights as well as you can. We've none for them to aim at. Let me get to that tube. It's of no use—but——"

There he paused, for the Spanish lights were drawing sensibly nearer.

On sped the propeller, nevetheless, and another warning gun rang out from the enemy.

"All accident," said Jack, "but it went right over us. I do believe I have their range. What? A broadside?"

They had his range, too, remarkably, for more than one shot struck the Lincoln as he fired. All were of moderate weight, however, and only one of them exploded.

"Well, there's no one below!" exclaimed Mike. "That bust among the cargo. It went through, somehow."

"Our shot exploded! It hit 'em!" triumphantly responded Jack. "I wish I knew what harm it did. Now, Robinson, if you have the range, fire!"

"Aye, aye! May be I have. There!"

The forward tube spoke out, and to the astonishment of everybody that torpedo also must have struck, for its thundering explosion came back ominously across the water.

"So very near!" said Esmeralda.

"I'm goin' below," said Mike, "to take a look."

But at that moment there was dire consternation on board their enemy, with too many lights showing.

"The propeller gone? The rudder?" exclaimed her commander, in dismay.

"It's the very pirate we chased in. She carries heavy guns! We are ruined! Hit forward?"

"At the water line," excitedly responded one of his officers. Another such hole would sink us. Nobody killed or wounded."

"We can't follow if we wanted to," said his commander. "But that fellow can't escape the cruiser. All hands repair ship!"

That was precisely the order that needed to be given on board the Lincoln also. Not at the water line, but a few feet above it, one of the steel plates had been shattered by the shell from the Spaniard. Patching could be done, of course, but the propeller would be in hardly as good trim for a heavy gale. At all events, the next few minutes declared that she was no longer followed, and the near neighborhood of the islands compelled her to slow up.

The moon arose to help, and showed them patches of white surf and of forest-covered keys to be avoided. Painfully waned the night, and when the dawn came all were eagerly watching the increasing light with something of silent dread.

"Esmeralda," exclaimed Jack, "we are out in the Caribbean Sea, and there is not a sail in sight. We are safe!"

"Thank God!" she said, and every other pair of lips seemed to be saying the same words.

After long tension of excitement there is apt to be a calm. Well for the damaged propeller that the sea itself was disposed to be peaceable during the next few days.

Not in the comfortless roadstead off the Mexican port of Vera Cruz, but into one of the muddy channels of the delta of the Mississippi did the adventurous propeller thrust her nose, nobody hindering. She found a place, too, at the New Orleans levee, and the proper officers boarded her to make the customary inquiries.

"From New York for Vera Cruz? Put in here damaged to discharge cargo?" inquired an intelligent looking custom house official of Jack. "Got hurt in the storm? Poor fellow! Big wave stove a hole! Yes! Always so. Hope you landed everything all right and gave 'em something! Papers all right, sir. Don't say anything just yet. Billy McKinley is getting ready as fast as he can. So am I. I'm in. Remember the Maine! Glad you put your guns all down in the hold, though, so I needn't know they are there. Hurrah for Free Cuba!"

So the whole affair was kept a profound secret, and nobody, not even the customhouse officers so much as guessed that the Lincoln was an anti-Spanish pirate.

There were telegrams to send and receive, however, and only a day later Commodore Vanderheyden remarked to a friend of his, confidentially:

"That propeller of mine! I'm proud of her. Regular gunboat. Torpedo tubes are first rate for her kind. I'm proud of Jack, too. He's going to marry her at New Orleans and fetch her north. Then, as soon as his arm is well and war is declared, he says he is going out after Spaniards. I'll give the Lincoln to Uncle Sam. Hurrah for the stars and stripes!''

THE END.

PRINTED BY R. R. DONNELLEY
AND SONS COMPANY AT THE
LAKESIDE PRESS, CHICAGO, ILL.

By HAROLD FREDERIC

GLORIA MUNDI: A NOVEL

Mr. Frederic's two triumphs of the last few years have been "The Damnation of Theron Ware" in serious fiction and "March Hares" in a light and brilliantly witty style which is all his own. "Gloria Mundi" comes as his first work since the publication of these two successful books—and happily enough —it combines the keen thoughtful analysis of the one with the delicacy of touch of the other. Mr. Frederic takes for his hero a young man brought up without much attention in the south of France, who, by a wholly unexpected combination of circumstances, falls heir to an English earldom. His entire training has unfitted him for the position, and Mr. Frederic makes much of the difficulties it forces upon him. The other characters are some good and bad members of the nobility, an "actress-lady," and a type-writer.

12mo. Cloth. Uniform with "The Damnation of Theron Ware." $1.50.

THE DAMNATION OF THERON WARE

It is unnecessary at this time to say much of "The Damnation of Theron Ware" or "Illumination" as it is called in England. The sales have already reached thirty-five thousand, which is in itself the most substantial evidence of the novel's readable-ness. Owing to the failure of its former publishers the book was temporarily out of print, but it is now enjoying a constant and certain success.

The merit of the book is worthy of special praise because of the exceptional strength, variety, and originality of the char-acters. —*Cleveland World.*

Mr. Frederic has written a daring story, and one which is doubly impressive because of the straightforward simplicity of his manner of presenting his case. His attack is certainly a bold one, and it will be strange if he does not bring down the unani-mous maledictions of the cloth on his devoted head.—*Chicago Evening Post.*

12mo. Cloth. Thirty-fifth thousand. $1.50.

HERBERT S. STONE & CO., CHICAGO & NEW YORK.

By H. C. CHATFIELD-TAYLOR

THE VICE OF FOOLS

A novel of society life in Washington.

The great success of Mr. Chatfield-Taylor's society novels gives assurance of a large sale to this new story. It can hardly be denied that few persons in this country are better qualified to treat the "smart set" in various American cities, and the life in diplomatic circles offers an unusually picturesque opportunity.

Mr. Chatfield-Taylor has brought out a fourth novel, and one which is distinctly a gain in style over his previous achievements in that line. As a series of society scenes the panorama of the book is perfect. A dinner at the Hungarian embassy is detailed with much humor, great pictorial power and keen knowledge. The dialogue may be characterized heartily as crisp, witty, and sparkling. Mr. Chatfield-Taylor proves himself a past master of epigram; and if society were to talk a tenth as well as he represents there would be no cause for accusing it of frivolity.— *Chicago Times-Herald.*

16mo. Cloth. With ten full-page illustrations by Raymond M. Crosby. Fifth thousand. $1.50.

TWO WOMEN AND A FOOL

The story of an actress, an artist and a very sweet girl. The scenes are laid in Chicago, London, and Paris; in theatres, studios, and bachelor apartments. It is the history of an infatuation—with moral interludes.

Mr. H. C. Chatfield-Taylor, whom Paul Bourget has named as the most promising novelist of American social life, has given us a clever story in "Two Women and a Fool." The tale is retrospective; one hears it from the lips of Guy, an artist; and it concerns his love for two women, a very naughty and an extremely nice one, Moira and Dorothy respectively. Moira, who becomes a soubrette, leads Guy, who becomes a successful artist, a tremendous pace, wearying him at length, but still holding the power to revive him with her look that allures. The romance leaps from Chicago to London and Paris and back to the Windy City again. It is steadily entertaining, and its dialogue, which is always witty, is often brilliant. C. D. Gibson's pictures are really illustrative.—*Philadelphia Press.*

18mo. Cloth. With frontispiece by C. D. Gibson. Ninth thousand. $0.75.

HERBERT S. STONE & CO., CHICAGO & NEW YORK.

By JULIA MAGRUDER

A REALIZED IDEAL

Miss Julia Magruder has by this time firmly established her reputation as one of the most popular of our younger writers. Many readers had their introduction to her when "The Princess Sonia" began in the pages of *The Century Magazine*, and all agreed that the most charming love-story they had read for years came from this almost unknown Southern girl.

Since then "The Violet" and a volume of short stories, entitled, "Miss Ayr of Virginia," have appeared. In the title of this latest volume, Miss Magruder, in a way, makes the confession that she is an old-fashioned writer. At least she is not modern in some of the unpleasant meanings of the word. In her book, "ideals" are sometimes to be "realized," and the whole story is an unobtrusive protest in favor of sweetness and of sentiment in fiction.

The volume is bound in an exceedingly good design by Frank Hazenplug, in three colors.

16mo. Cloth. $1.25.

MISS AYR OF VIRGINIA AND OTHER STORIES

By means of original incident and keen portraiture, "Miss Ayr of Virginia, and Other Stories," is made a decidedly readable collection. In the initial tale the character of the young Southern girl is especially well drawn; Miss Magruder's most artistic work, however, is found at the end of the volume, under the title "Once More."—*The Outlook*.

The contents of "Miss Ayr of Virginia" are not less fascinating than the cover. * * * These tales * * * are a delightful diversion for a spare hour. They are dreamy without being candidly realistic, and are absolutely refreshing in the simplicity of the author's style.—*Boston Herald*.

Julia Magruder's stories are so good that one feels like reading passages here and there again and again. In the collection, "Miss Ayr of Virginia and Other Stories," she is at her best, and "Miss Ayr of Virginia," has all the daintiness, the point and pith and charm which the author so well commands. The portraiture of a sweet, unsophisticated, pretty, smart Southern girl is bewitching.—*Minneapolis Times*.

With a cover designed by F. R. Kimbrough. 16mo. $1.25.

HERBERT S. STONE & CO., CHICAGO & NEW YORK.

www.ingramcontent.com/pod-product-compliance
Lightning Source LLC
Chambersburg PA
CBHW060538030726
47498CB00004B/1241